Bradley Farm

Bradley Farm Series
Book 1

MARY JANE FORBES

Todd Book Publications

Bradley Farm

This is a work of fiction. All of the characters, names, locations,
incidents, organizations, and dialogue in this novel are either the
products of the author's imagination or are used fictitiously. The
views expressed in this work are solely those of the author.

ISBN: 978-0692436561 (sc)
Printed in the United States of America
Todd Book Publications: 4/2015
Port Orange, Florida

Author photo: Geri Rogers
Cover design 2018 by Angie: pro_ebookcovers

Books by Mary Jane Forbes

DroneKing Trilogy
A Toy for Christmas, A Ghostly Affair
Love is in the Air

Bradley Farm Series
Bradley Farm, Sadie,
Jeli, Marshall, Georgie

The Baker Girl Series
One Summer, Promises

Twists of Fate Series
The Fisherman, a love story
The Witness, living a lie
Twists of Fate

Murder by Design, Series
Murder by Design
Labeled in Seattle
Choices, And the Courage to Risk

Novels
The Mailbox, Black Magic,
The Painter, Twister

The Baby Quilt, The Message

House of Beads Mystery Series
Murder in the House of Beads
Intercept, Checkmate
Identity Theft

Short Stories
Once Upon a Christmas Eve, a Romantic Fairy Tale
The Christmas Angel and the Magic Holiday Tree
RJ, The Little Hero

Visit: www.MaryJaneForbes.com

Bradley Farm

Part I
Chapter 1

Halloween, 1969

RAGGEDY ANN SAT on the top row of the bleachers in the high school's gymnasium. Orange and black crepe paper twisted into garlands draped from one ceiling girder to the next. A mirrored ball, hanging from the ceiling, slowly turned with the rising heat from the students vigorously dancing the Frug. The three-tiered set of bleachers on one side of the gym held groups of three or more girls who preferred to sit out the dance, or weren't asked by boys too shy to ask a girl to dance.

Costumes assembled from miniskirts as well as a scattering of the latest craze, long bohemian skirts, were worn by girls looking adoringly into their partner's eyes. The hippie era, born during the Woodstock Music and Art Festival, was embraced and embellished in this small high school on the outskirts of Exeter, New Hampshire.

Raggedy Ann, Jane O'Neill, fingered the white bow at the end of her red braid. Her fiery hair complemented her costume—white, lace-trimmed apron over a navy blue, short-sleeved cotton dress that graced the top of a pair of red and white striped knee highs. Raggedy Ann sat alone on one end of the bleachers, toes of her black Mary Jane's turned in, her free hand gripping the edge of the bleacher. Her gaze was fixed on the band. A five-piece student group formed by Daniel Bradley. Last year, a leap year, Jane was going to ask Danny to be her date at the school's Sadie Hawkins dance. But when she bumped into him after English class, she suddenly became tongue-tied and ran to her next class.

• • •

AFTER THAT FATEFUL DAY, Danny Bradley had sought Jane out in the school library. Danny's mind was always spinning from one thing to the next, thinking about what he wanted to do with his life on the farm, definitely learn new ways to help his dad with the land. While he was quick to grasp the plays as quarterback and captain of the football team, and quick to perform his duties on the farm, it seemed he never had enough time to study for his classes. The A he wanted to achieve remained elusive, so he settled for Bs and even an occasional C. He was horrified when he got a D in math. Something had to be done. Fearing failure of any kind, he set a high-bar for himself, a bar that always seemed just out of reach.

Jane O'Neill was known for her straight As, so he decided to approach her, ask her to help him with his studies. Stammering at his unexpected request, she said, "Sure. Yes."

Surprising his parents with an A in math on his next report card, he expanded his request for tutoring from the perky redhead. Now, at the Halloween dance, he decided he wanted to spend more time with Jane and not just in the library.

• • •

IT WAS TIME for the musicians to take a break. The band laid down their instruments and headed out of the gym for the punch bowl and cookies. Jane watched Danny follow the group to the door but when he looked up, saw her, he changed direction.

Priscilla, everyone called her Cilla, caught his arm, engaging him in conversation. Cilla was Jane's best friend because Cilla declared it so, wheedling Jane's help to pass her English finals. However, if Jane was going to be truthful, Jane didn't care much for her *best friend*. Cilla was bossy, didn't care about school, and was boy crazy. On every count, Jane was none of these things.

Jane, elbows on her knees, cupped her cheeks and watched the pair. Jane always felt that Danny preferred pretty Priscilla and wished she had Cilla's silky blonde hair instead of her mop of red. Maybe then Danny would talk to her instead of Cilla. Jane's heart was heavy whenever she saw Danny talking to any girl. She knew it was dumb but she couldn't help it.

Raggedy Ann watched Danny walk away from Cilla, leaving her with her hands on her hips and a sour look on her face. Danny walked along the front row of the bleachers, looked up and smiled as he mounted the tiered seats.

"Hi, Jane."

"Hi … hi, Danny."

"Are you having fun?"

"Sure."

"What do you think of my band, well, kinda my band?"

"You're wonderful … ah, the band is wonderful. I like your pirate costume. Does the mustache tickle?"

"A little. I had to take the skull and crossbones hat off. Kept falling over my eyes."

"How did you learn to play so many instruments? I mean, the harmonica, the guitar, flute…

"My grandfather. He even played the horn, the drums … mom laid down the law. No drums for me. Too much racket she said."

"That's amazing."

"I guess I inherited the genes from my father's side. Mom doesn't play anything. She says, 'someone has to work around here,'" Danny said mimicking his mother's voice.

"I play the piano … a little. Not professional like you play your instruments."

"Jane, after the group starts up again, I can slip away for a song. Would you like to dance?"

"Oh, I don't … I can't … dance very well …

"No problem. I have heavy shoes on," he said picking up her hand. A smile spread across his tanned face, tanned from the hours spent on the football field.

Jane scrunched her brows. "What…

"In case you step on my toes." Danny laughed. "I see the guys coming back. After three numbers I'll look for you up here. Okay?"

"Okay."

Danny dropped her hand and hurried back to the band. He lifted his guitar, tapped his toe, strummed a bar and then the four other boys joined in—drums, keyboard and two more guitars.

Jane hurried out of the gym to the girl's restroom. Cilla on Jane's heels burst through the door after her. "You looked pretty chummy with Danny Bradley. Of course, he talked to me first. I can't believe it. Did you ask him to dance?"

"He asked me. I wouldn't have …

"Well, next time I see him leave the band I'm going to ask him to dance. You back off."

Jane didn't tell her *best friend* that Danny had already asked her to dance and that he'd find her. Drying her hands, Jane left for the refreshments.

Fruit punch and sugar cookies decorated with black and orange piped icing, were lined up on folding tables in the wide hallway outside the gym. Napkins with pumpkins, skull and crossbones, or ghosts, fanned out around the punch bowl. Mothers and fathers, undercover chaperones, helped with the refreshments. The Halloween dance was the first of many events planned for the students celebrating their senior year.

Picking up a cookie, a chaperone smiled at Jane, handing her a napkin. "Having a good time, Jane?"

Jane smiled. "I am thank you."

"You make a perfect Raggedy Ann with your red pigtails."

"Thanks."

Jane climbed to the top of the bleachers, sat in the same place where Danny had found her before. *I wonder if he meant it. Dance with me?*

The kids were dancing fast, arms and legs flailing about performing the Chicken, another dance craze spawned by the Twist.

Her heart seized when Danny said something to the boy holding a guitar next to him. They nodded to each other and he left the band. He looked up at her in the bleachers, smiled, and began walking toward her. Jane could see Cilla hurrying from the opposite direction to catch him, but Danny was already climbing the bleachers, walking along the third-row plank to her. "Will you dance with me, Jane?" He stood towering over her, offering her his hand.

Smiling, she put her hand in his, and followed him down the bleachers.

On the dance floor, Danny picked up her hand, put his arm around her waist, smiled into her green eyes as he led her to the slow music.

Jane had never been held the way Danny was holding her. Close. So close she caught the scent of his cologne.

"Would you like to go to the movies next Saturday?" he asked his cheek against her cheek.

She didn't answer.

He leaned away, looked down into her big eyes, red pigtails framing her face as she lifted her eyes to share his gaze. "Sure. I'd like to. Thanks for asking."

"I'll pick you up, if that's okay with your folks. You let me know if it's okay. I'll call. Hold on a second. Here," he said pulling a piece of paper from his pants pocket along with a stub of a pencil. "Here's my number." Danny tore the slip of paper in half handing her both pieces. "You write your number. I'll call you, but in case you want to call me, you'll have my number too. I think the evening show starts at seven. Tell your folks I'll have you home by ten o'clock. That will give us time to have a soda. Okay?"

She nodded, smiling.

Danny asked her to dance once more, and then it was time to leave. Her father would be waiting and she didn't want to get a lecture on promptness. The band began packing up their instruments. Jane saw Danny slip his harmonica into his pocket as she turned away, felt his eyes following her to the outside exit, following her as she pushed the bar on the heavy gym door.

A blast of cold air hit her face but she didn't notice. Her body was still warm from Danny's arms holding her as they danced. Mr. O'Neill propped open the car door and Jane slipped in beside him.

Reality hit her. *Stupid. Stupid. Stupid.* She yanked the door shut and her father pulled away from the curb, turning out of the long school driveway onto the street.

Glancing at his daughter, he asked, "Have fun?"

"I'm an idiot. Idiot. Idiot," she whispered.

"Jane, you are not an idiot. What happened?"

What should she say? She didn't want to stir up trouble … telling him, even hinting that she liked a boy. Not any boy. Daniel Bradley, the captain of the football team.

"Did you dance?"

"Oh, yes. Three times."

"And…

"And Daniel Bradley asked me to the movies on Saturday. Said he'd pick me up if it's alright with you and Mother."

"We met Mr. and Mrs. Bradley at a parent-teacher conference last spring. Stuffy man. Runs a farm. Horse farm, I think he said. Races horses. Word has it he loses more than he wins. Check if it's alright with your mother. You have to be back by ten."

Jane let the subject drop. Her father seemed intent on the road and she was going to leave it that way. *I'm such a dunce. I barely said a word. I'm sure he'll find me after class on Monday with some excuse to cancel his invitation.*

"Just remember, don't get tied up with a boy. You're going to college. And, we may be moving by next spring … definitely by summer. My company is making plans to expand and they want me to head up the accounting group. Big promotion for me."

"Moving? Where?"

"Los Angeles."

No. No. No. Raggedy Ann's eyes bulged as she stared out the side window, tall trees silhouetted in the moon whizzing in and out of sight, mocking her. She couldn't breathe. *My senior year? Danny asked me to dance tonight. Maybe he won't cancel the movie date. I can't move away now.*

● ● ●

MONDAY'S CLASSES DRAGGED. Cilla asked her several times if she was okay. Was she sick?

Danny didn't cancel.

On Friday, after English, Danny sidled up to her walking down the hall. *Here it comes,* she thought. *The big, SORRY, I didn't really mean to ask you to the movies.*

"Everything okay for the movies tomorrow? Your mom and dad … okay with me picking you up?"

"Yes, they're fine. They met your parents last spring."

"Great. I checked what's playing—Butch Cassidy and the Sundance Kid, or The Wonderful Land of Oz. Thought maybe you'd like a musical—singing, dancing." He smiled at her as he said it.

He wasn't canceling. Jane stopped short, looked up at the handsome captain of the football team, his black wavy hair circling his ears. "Danny, that is incredibly sweet of you. I love Streisand, but I think Butch Cassidy would be great. It's had rave reviews."

"Butch Cassidy it is. Pick you up at 7:00 tomorrow night. How did you do on that English exam?"

"Perfect score. A plus."

"I think I'd better coerce you into being my tutor in English as well as math. See you tomorrow."

Jane smiled after him. "Tomorrow."

Chapter 2

———

THE PREVIOUSLY-OWNED red truck, spit and polished, rolled down the street of the tidy tree-lined neighborhood. Craning his neck to read the house numbers, Danny pulled up in front of the O'Neill's mid-sized red brick house set back from the sidewalk. Eagerly hopping out of his red 4 by 4, he trotted up to the front door and punched the doorbell. Straightening his football letter sweater over khaki trousers, he waited for Jane to answer the bell.

A man opened the door, a man Danny took to be Jane's father with a woman standing behind him. The man glanced out at the truck then back at the boy standing on the other side of the screen door grinning back at him—a boy with a shock of black hair grazing his brows but trimmed on the side, a boy with a quiet air of confidence.

"Hi, I'm Daniel Bradley. I'm here to pick up Jane."

"Come in, Daniel. I'm Jane's father. She'll be right down. Daniel this is Jane's mother, Mrs. O'Neill."

The woman standing behind her husband stepped up. "Nice to meet you, Daniel."

"I don't know if she told you," Mr. O'Neill said, "but she has a ten o'clock curfew. We expect her to be home at that time."

"No problem, Mr. O'Neill. I'll make sure she's home by ten," Danny said grinning at Jane's parents.

Jane came running down the stairs, a tight grip on the banister to prevent a trip-and-fall entrance. The skirt of her dark green dress flipped with each step, a beige jacket over her arm. "Hi, Danny. I'm ready. You met my mother and father?"

"Yes, I did," Danny said nodding to each of the O'Neill's. He bumped open the screen door, holding it for Jane.

"Bye," Jane called over her shoulder as she breezed by her parents.

Danny held the truck door giving Jane a hand up. Certain she was settled, he scooted around sliding in behind the wheel.

Driving the few blocks into town, Danny kept eyeing Jane. "You look so pretty. I checked—the movie isn't quite two hours, so I think we'll have time for a soda. Kinda chilly out … maybe a hot chocolate?"

She glanced back at him with a quick smile. "That sounds about right. Do you like western films? The wild west?"

Danny slapped the steering wheel. "Love them. You are something else, Miss Jane O'Neill. Not many girls would ask me that. My dad raises race horses. He wears a black hat that is definitely wild west, cowboy like. I mimic him a lot. I have a tan cowboy hat just like his. So, yes, I like the wild west. A long way away from New Hampshire, though."

Jane looked out the side window. What else did the magazine article suggest? Oh yes, ask about what he dreams of doing … like after they graduate from school. Already, she was breathing at more or less a normal rate.

● ● ●

EMERGING FROM THE THEATRE into the chilly night air, Jane wrapped her jacket tighter against the breeze. Danny held her hand as they walked to the magazine and newspaper shop across the street. The soda fountain was part of the shop—split right down the center of the building. Scooting into the shop ahead of the other moviegoers straggling out of the theatre, Danny headed for the booth in the back, his head bobbing in rhythm to the movie's soundtrack playing from the jukebox. Dropping her hand, they slid into the booth sitting opposite each other. Warm and cozy. The waitress strolled up to the pair, pulling the order pad from her starched blue bib apron.

"Hi, Danny. What can I get for you two tonight?" she asked her foot tapping to the music, pen poised over the little pad.

Danny leaned toward Jane. "What will it be, Janie? Hot chocolate or chocolate soda?"

"Hot chocolate, please, Danny," Jane said grinning. She had often thought Janie would be a cute nickname, but no one had ever called her Janie until tonight.

"Two hot chocolates, please," Danny said looking up at the waitress who had no idea why the couple had funny grins on their faces.

The booths filled up quickly, as well as the red-vinyl covered stools at the counter. Chatter, laughter, mixed with an occasional shriek over a scene in the movie, filled the soda fountain and newspaper shop.

"Do you mind if I call you Janie? Because if you don't like—"

"I don't mind it a bit, Danny," Jane said with yet another grin.

"So, Janie, what are you going to do after we graduate?"

Her brows hitched up. Maybe he read the same magazine suggesting topics to talk about on a date.

"I want to be a teacher—young kids. I love kids."

"Ahh. I love kids too. Always thought it would be fun to play with brothers and sisters. Not much time on a farm to play with other kids."

"I know what you mean. I'm an only child...hoped for siblings, but ...

"Which campus?"

"The main one, Durham. But ...

"I've seen that one ... brochures. Very nice. Would you live on campus?"

"I guess. I don't know ... haven't been accepted yet." A chill ran up Jane's arm. Her father's words shooting into her head— *they might move*. The magazine warned of disappointment with a first date. So far this first date was not a disappointment. Danny was attentive, courteous. He went out of his way to please her. "Okay, your turn, Danny. What's in your future? College?"

"Nah. I'll be staying home, help my mom and dad with the farm. It's a big job … running the farm. When Dad goes to an event, like say, Saratoga in racing season, Mom shoulders all the responsibility. Something is always happening on the farm to stress them out. Dad breeds horses. Clients come to him with their mare or stallion to breed with another horse being trucked to our farm. Dad handles the breeding. Mom does all the paperwork—registration, the bloodline—stuff like that. Very important the registration is done correctly. The record of the breeding follows the horse through its life. Racing, and winning, means more money in future breeding—fees asked, and potential sale of the horses and their offspring."

"Wow. That's a lot of responsibility for you, your mom and dad. Do you have help? Employees?"

"We do. Farm hands. Lately times have been tough. Dad had to let two go. Told them when things turn around, after the next race, he'll hire them back. There's always a next race."

"Is that what you want to do … stay on the farm?"

"Never really thought about it as a question. I guess I just assumed that's what I'd do. There's a lot of alone time, out in the fields. Maybe I'll write songs. Send them to Glen Campbell. He sings cowboy songs. Then there's my woodworking."

"Like what?"

"Mom says I could make a living at it—simple stuff, like a stool she can put her feet up on at the end of a busy day. Built a small stand for the kitchen—dowels for handles to hold her kitchen towels. She loved it. But what I really like to do is carve, whittle, when I take a break in the hayfields. Would you like to come over sometime? See the farm? Meet my mom and dad?"

"Can I see your carving?"

"That can be arranged."

"Then, yes, I'd like that very much."

A group of boys filing out of the soda fountain slapped each other on the back, laughing at a private joke. Jane watched them.

They didn't have a care in the world. "My mother keeps the house in order. My father is an accountant for a company in Portsmouth."

"What's the matter, Janie?"

Jane reverted her stare from the boys leaving back to Danny, her face blank, except for a slight furrowing of her brows.

"You look like something is bothering you."

"My father said his company is opening a branch next year."

"Where?"

"Los Angeles."

"Oh … Janie, can you come to the farm this Saturday … or Sunday would be better. I have football practice Saturday morning. I'd really like you to see it—the land, the house and barns.

"Sunday is good. My father …

"I'll pick you up. Do you go to church?"

"Yes … St. Mary's down the street. I could meet you out front. 12:15?"

"I'll be waiting out front. 12:15."

Chapter 3

———

ANOTHER DATE? Same boy? Jane's parents both sucked up air, expelling in a rush from open mouths. They were not happy when she told them that Danny was picking her up after church to take her to the farm, show her around, and to meet his mom and dad. That farm boy was not good enough for their daughter but they held their tongues. After all, they would be moving next summer, maybe as early as spring.

The parishioners filed out of the church into the bright November sunshine, the mild temperature along with the minister's sermon warming all hearts. Jane dressed conservatively in a knee-length navy blue dress. Swinging her tote over her shoulder, she waved to the boy standing by the red truck.

"Be home before dark, young lady," her mother said through pinched lips.

Jane called over her shoulder that she would, as she trotted up to Danny holding the truck door open, giving her a hand up. He squinted in the bright sun at her parents, gave them a friendly wave, and then climbed behind the wheel.

"You're pretty as a picture again, Janie. You'll have to step carefully in those shoes when I show you around the farm but don't worry, I'll guide you." He smiled at her, then turned back to the road. *Yes siree, pretty as a picture.*

Jane patted her tote. "Not to worry, Danny. I brought a change of clothes—T-shirt, jeans and sneakers. I suspected there might be some hazards out in the field," Jane said with a little giggle.

"I have to warn you, just in case Mom says something. It's my birthday today so she'll probably bake a cake—"

"Daniel Bradley, your birthday? You never said—"

"I know. I didn't want a fuss, but you know how moms are. Besides, she cooks up a mean three-layer chocolate cake."

"Your favorite?"

"Nothing like chocolate, Janie."

The ride was short. A few miles out of town Danny turned into a long driveway. The stout signpost at the road marked the entrance—Bradley Horse Farm.

"You sit tight. I'll come around, help you down. It's a big step," Danny said as he slid off the truck seat.

Jane nodded but her attention was riveted on his house. It was huge—white clapboard, gray roof with several dormers—a window in each peak on the second floor, or was it the third floor. The roofline had many angles with a graceful slope to a large extension on the left side. A granite rock retaining wall bordered a sloping lawn leading up to the front of the house. A profusion of colorful bushes and clumps of flowers surrounded the house.

"Danny ...

Her words trailed off as two, no three huge red barns came into view. Raising her hand to her eyes, she saw another barn off in the distance—a soft yellow—or was it a small house?

"Here comes Dad. He's anxious to meet you. I probably won't get a word in edgewise when we go to the horse barn," he said helping Jane out of the truck.

"I know nothing about horses, Danny, but that is one big animal he's riding."

Danny laughed. "You can say that again. But he sure can run. He's won us a lot of money. His name is Sir Charles."

Danny's dad pulled up his horse several feet from the truck, handed the reins to his son, and approached Jane.

"Well, my son wasn't joking. You *are* pretty. Wherever did you get that red hair?" he asked sticking out his hand, a broad smile under twinkling eyes.

Smiling back, Jane placed her small hand into his large calloused palm. She could see where Danny got his good looks—wavy coal black hair peeked out from a black cowboy hat shading dark brown eyes, a muscular frame. He wore a pair of khaki trousers, matching shirt. Dark brown cowboy boots anchored him. A charmer. Like father like son. She immediately liked him.

"Happy to meet you, Mr. Bradley. Your home, the barns … everything is beautiful."

"Please, call me Arnie."

He turned as a dog, a Bassett hound mix, came rushing up the path on short stumpy legs, feet pointing out, barking punctuated with nose-in-the-air howls, coming to an abrupt stop in front of Arnie. "Jane, meet Suzy," he said fishing a biscuit out of his pocket, and then signaled the dog to sit. Suzy carefully accepted her treat, then shifted, tail sweeping the ground, to Danny who gave her another biscuit. Shifting again, Suzy faced Jane, raising her head with a soft bark.

"Suzy, you're such a beggar. Here, Jane. Give her this or she'll pester the life out of you."

Jane accepted the biscuit from Arnie which Suzy carefully took from her delicate fingers, laying her long silky ears back as Jane gingerly stroked her head. She'd never had a dog and wasn't sure what to do but Suzy seemed to accept her.

"Where's Mom?"

"Up at the house. Fixing Sunday dinner, I think, and frosting a certain chocolate cake. Show Jane around, son. I'll meet you at the horse barn."

"Didn't I tell you?" Danny said taking Jane's hand. "We'll stop at the mudroom—this end of the house. The red door. You can change and then be prepared for a hike. We have two-hundred acres to roam. While you're changing I'll tell Mom where we're going and that we'll be raring for Sunday dinner in a couple of hours."

Horse Barn

IT WAS A PERFECT DAY for a hike. Jane held fast to Danny's hand as her eyes darted from one barn to the other, one field to the other—a scattering of pumpkins, a few Christmas trees, fields dotted with hay bales. Jane sighed, deeply inhaling the sweet smell of fresh hay, then the scent of pine needles. The farm was alive in every corner, so much to take in. She didn't notice the barns needed a coat of paint or that the training track was glutted with weeds.

Next, Danny guided her to the horse barn. Arnie was standing outside by a big brown horse, a tad smaller than Sir Charles but a much broader chest.

"What do you think, Jane ... of the farm, Mildred here, and of course, Sir Charles?"

A grin spread across her face. Mr. Bradley was a proud man and very proud of his horses.

"Mr. Bradley, the farm ... more than I can ever see in a day. Does Mildred race?"

"No, no." Stroking the white blaze on Mildred's nose, he laughed. "She's a worker. Keeps the farm going. Pulled out an ornery stump in the middle of a hay field a few years ago. Here's an apple. Give it to her and you'll be her friend for life," he said polishing the apple on his shirt.

"Will she bite me?"

"Never. Hold it out so she can reach it."

Jane took the shiny red apple from him, held it out to Mildred. The mare gently wrapped her large lips around the treat, chomped, then whinnied for another.

"Come on, Jane, let me show you what we do here."

"Dad, did the stallion show up yesterday while I was at practice?"

"Oh, sure did. Big guy. The mare is waiting. We'll get the two together after you take Jane home. Don't want to show her everything the first visit."

Arnie pulled the heavy barn door on creaky hinges opening the stall area. Stepping inside he took Jane on a tour—the tack room filled with brushes, hooks holding bridles, leather straps of all sorts, shelves of liniment along with large and small jars and tins. A chalkboard was mounted on the wall listing what had to be done before breeding the visitors. A space heater, rocking chair with a frayed pad and a stool for Arnie to put his feet up for a rest were tucked in the corner.

Arnie flipped on his eight-track cassette player. "Nothing like a little Louie Armstrong ... Ella Fitzgerald to get the horses in the mood for a good brushing. I swear, when I turn on the player they know it's grooming time."

"I like Satchmo. Jazz. Danny played a trumpet at the Halloween dance," Jane said. "Did you teach him?"

"Nah. He picked it up by himself. Of course, it comes in his genes—my dad, his dad."

They ambled back to the main wide area of the barn bordered by stalls—Sir Charles at one end and Mildred at the other end. The two stalls in the middle were empty as were the stalls along the opposite wall. Stepping outside Arnie pointed to his right. "Up the hill you can see another small barn for a stallion such as the one dropped off yesterday. He's kept separate from the mare or mares as the case may be. The mares are housed in yet another barn with a lean-to shed when breeding occurs. I hear some breeders are trying artificial insemination but it's not a common practice around here … might be some day in the future. The new method of breeding protects the horses from getting hurt."

Sheltering his eyes from the sun, Danny pointed to a large fenced oval track. "That's where Dad used to train Sir Charles for the next big race."

"Do you still race him, Arnie?"

"No. He's had his glory days."

Chapter 4

———

Farmhouse Kitchen

FATHER AND SON sauntered with Jane back to the house. Danny held Jane's hand, which did not go unnoticed by his dad. A woman was standing at the red mudroom door, arms hugging her chest to ward off the cool late afternoon air. Her white flowered apron with a profusion of purple forget-me-nots was tied around her thick waist. A spot of chocolate frosting had dropped on the apron's pocket.

As they approached, Arnie called out to her. "Martha, we've worked up a powerful appetite. I hope you cooked up a good batch of spuds to go with that leg of lamb, and no fretting. There's always room for chocolate cake."

Martha didn't look happy as she fixed her eyes on Jane. Jane felt a sudden chill. Danny's mom didn't seem to have his father's easy-going, friendly demeanor. Her brown hair, streaked with gray, was held back in a bun accentuating her stern look.

"Janie, I'd like you to meet my mom. Mom, this is Jane."

Jane nervously stuck out her hand, "Happy to meet you, Mrs. Bradley."

Martha gave a pump to the smooth, white hand offered to her, nodded, turned to her husband. "Better check the root cellar. Something's knocking down there again."

"Martha, I've checked that cellar so many times, the stairs are worn out."

"Well, open up the outside hatch. You won't have to turn on the light with the angle of the sun."

Suzy began to whine, slinking on her belly behind Danny.

Jane's brows furrowed, questioning. She looked from Mrs. Bradley to Mr. Bradley to Suzy then up to Danny.

"Here, Dad, I'll give you a hand."

Arnie pulled a ring of keys out of his pocket, selected one and opened the padlock, pulled up the hasp. Then father and son strained to lift the heavy, weather-beaten wooden hatch. The rotting wooden planks creaked on rusty hinges as Arnie grasped a handrail of sorts, a small section of a tree fastened to the top and bottom of the haphazard, rickety wooden steps.

Suddenly, a mangy, curly, yellow-haired dog the size of a bear cub, shot in front of Danny, leaping down to the floor of the cellar.

He stood quivering, barking.

Still barking, he began digging frantically, possessed, his paws clawing at the dirt. Danny climbed down the planks, stood beside his father watching the frenzied animal, a mound of dirt piling up around his hind legs. Still, the dog continued to dig.

An object, dirty, yellowed, began to surface.

A skull.

Whining, the dog laid down, tongue hanging out, panting. A whoosh of air swirled around the man and the boy, their hair grazing the low ceiling floorboards of the kitchen above. The whoosh escaped up and out of the cellar's hatch.

Both Mrs. Bradley and Jane, arms wrapped around their bodies against the sudden chill, peered down into the gaping hole of the cellar.

"Arnold, what's that dog doing? Come out of there. Danny, help your father."

"The dog dug something up, Mom …

"What? Come out of there, both of you. Arnold!"

Suzy cowered behind Martha, her big brown eyes peeking around Martha's heavy brown stocking-encased legs.

Arnie squatted, moved a small piece of rock, staring at the skull.

Danny squatted beside the dog, scratching him behind his ears. "It's okay, boy," he said, looking at the hollow eyes of the skull. "Dad, it's like the dog was waiting for us to open the trap door to the cellar. Who do you suppose it was?"

"I think we'd better join your mother. Have dinner. Then, maybe … maybe I'll call the police. They'll take it away."

"Can they tell if it's a man or a woman? Dad, maybe the dog is laying on top of the rest … the rest of the bones."

"Arnold, you come up here. You're scaring me. What are you looking at?"

"A skull," he called over his shoulder. "The dog dug up a skull."

Danny followed in his dad's footsteps as they climbed out of the cellar. The dog, squeezing out between them, laid on the ground as they closed the hatch, fastening the padlock.

Arnie looked down at the dog, dirt caked between its toes. "It's been almost a year, Martha, since that mutt came to our door. Fur still matted like before. Remember when he ran up to us. Danny was with us same as now, standing in the same spot. He barked and barked. Ran figure eights around us. An instant love affair—us and the dog. But you swore you didn't want another dog in the house after Eddie was hit by a snowplow. Suzy was enough you said. That was not a fun Christmas."

Suzy squirmed across the grass on her belly, whining, scrooching close beside the big dog.

"After dinner I'll take him to the barn, hose him down."

"Enough. Let's eat dinner," Martha said as she turned to the back door. "You tell me what you propose to do with the ... with the skull."

The men did most of the talking around the dinner table, the air filled with the tantalizing scents of Sunday dinner. Jane reveled in the way Martha had prepared the food. The lamb was the most succulent she ever ate. The carrots, Martha called copper pennies, melting in her mouth. Jane asked her where the name copper pennies came from.

"All I can say is that Arnie's mother made the dish and I believe her mother before. Medium carrots sliced thin like a copper penny, boiled briefly, drained. In a bowl she combined celery, green pepper, the carrots and onion. Then she mixed in tomato soup, oil, vinegar and sugar bringing the new mix to a boil, then refrigerated. She served the copper pennies as a salad or warm as a side dish."

"I like the way you served it ... as a salad," Jane said.

Martha cut the three-layer chocolate cake, carefully sliding a wedge on to each plate. Placing a plate in front of Danny, she looked up. "Happy birthday, son. Eighteen. A man."

"Thanks, Mom. Umm, delicious as always," he said leaning over, kissing her cheek.

Martha quickly removed a speck of dust from her eye, glanced at her husband. "Arnie, are you going to call the police?"

"Yes ... in the morning. The hatch is secure. The dog won't be going down there to dig for the rest of the skeleton, if there is one."

Chapter 5

―――

"I DON'T THINK your mother likes me, a city girl."

Danny winced inside. He knew his mother could be cool to strangers. He turned the truck out of the driveway on to the road leading into town. "She just takes a while to warm up to someone new. What did you think of the farm?"

Jane turned in the seat, straining against the seatbelt, a full smile spreading under her big green eyes. "Amazing. I've never seen anything like it. The hay bales, the barns, the horses." Jane laughed, "I didn't expect to see pumpkins dotting the fields."

"Did you see the one I put in the back of the truck for you?"

She craned her neck further. "Danny, it's huge."

"I'll carve it if you like. A jolly Jack-o-lantern from Bradley Horse Farm."

"I'd like that, except for one thing," she replied grinning. "Halloween's over."

Turning back in her seat, she stared out the side window at the leaves gathering at the bases of the maple, and birch trees, every now and then broken with a patch of lawn, a gate, a house.

"Well, there's always pumpkin pie. Mom roasts the seeds—a little salt. Yum."

"Your mom makes a pie from the pulp?"

"What do you think the cans in the grocery store are filled with, silly?"

"Do you think she'd part with the family recipe? I'd love to try it?"

"Of course, she would."

"You're like your dad, you know. Besides your looks—warm, friendly, easy to talk to. The football captain, the almost elected school president."

"Tommy campaigned harder than I did. He deserved to beat me."

"He wooed the girls. That's for sure. But I've seen another side of you as well, Mr. Bradley."

"You have? Like what?"

"The serious Daniel Bradley. The one who concentrates, intent on learning something new. The one who thinks he's failed if he doesn't get an A. Like what I showed you in math, for instance. You worked on it and pulled an A out of the class. That side of Daniel Bradley."

"Well, I saw another side of you today, too, Miss Janie O'Neill. A fun-loving Janie, curious about everything she saw. I laughed listening to you pepper Dad with questions about the horses, the farm."

"Oh, oh. I talked too much?"

"Not at all. He loved it."

Jane stared out the window, stared at the land preparing for winter. "Who do you think the … the skull belonged to? It was creepy, showing up like that. Gave me goose bumps."

"No idea. The house was built by my great, great, grandfather in 1840. I'm told the place was more of a dairy farm with crops to support cows for feed. It's rumored he had two wives, had twins with one of them. Dad was born in the house as were most of the Bradley family before him. When my grandfather died, the third Bradley, Dad took over the farm. He was already married to Mom. They've lived in the house from the time they were married. Grandmother died young—pneumonia, and then grandfather died of a heart attack. Dad says it was more of a broken heart. Dad loves horses, so as soon as he had pinched enough pennies together, he bought his first racehorse. A beauty—before Sir

Charles. He began breeding him, then others hired him to breed their stallion to someone else's mare. And so the business began. Slow at first, and then he made lots of money. But …

"But?"

"I can see the breeding business is tailing off … may be just a lull. I don't know. Anyway, now you've seen it and met my folks, Sir Charles, Suzy—and the excitement of a mystery skull. I wish you could come over for Thanksgiving dinner."

"My mother and father wouldn't hear of it. And, I'm not sure your mother would want me either. Do you have more family—aunts, uncles"?

"My dad's brother in Oregon. He's not well. And his sister lives in New Mexico. We're not close to them. They fled the farm after high school—wanted nothing to do with farming. Dad sees his sister when he races at Saratoga. But not if Mom's with him. She doesn't get along with his sister. Mom is too practical for my flighty aunt."

Chapter 6

―――

ARNIE WAVED AT DANNY as he drove off to school. Turning away from the window he polished off his second cup of coffee, reached for the phone, and punched in the number for his good friend and poker buddy.

"Hello, Chief Saxon, here."

"Good morning, Roy."

"Arnie, nice to hear from you. Not sure you would ever call again after my pair of aces beat your kings. Have a good weekend?"

"Yes, but I'm not calling to shoot the breeze about those lucky cards."

"What's up?"

"A mangy yellow dog dug up a skull in our root cellar yesterday."

"The root cellar? A skull … any other bones?"

"I don't know. The dog climbed out of the cellar exhausted. Thought I'd give you a ring. What am I supposed to do?"

"I'll send Goody out?"

"Goodman? What will he do? This isn't a corpse, Roy. Hardly needs the medical examiner."

"Well, I think we should try to find out who it was … unless you have an idea?"

"No, no. No idea."

"Quiet last night, no bodies brought in to the morgue. Goody can drive over to the farm in about an hour if that's okay with you. Gives him something to investigate, try out his forensic skills."

"An hour is fine. Gives me time to give Willie a list of chores at the horse barn."

"I thought you let Willie go?"

"I did, but I need his help with breeding a stallion that was dropped off Saturday. The mare is waiting, so to speak."

● ● ●

ARNIE WATCHED AS the medical examiner, squatting next to the skull, whisked away specs of dirt with a soft brush. "Can I use your phone, Mr. Bradley? I have to call in some lab techs to do some digging, check if there are more bones, maybe the skull belongs to what we can't see."

"Sure, come up to the house." Goodman followed Bradley out the trap door into the cold sunlight. The ME called the morgue for assistance, explaining what they should bring to excavate in the small space, or at least to check if there is a skeleton buried in the cellar.

"Coffee, Dr. Goodman?"

"Right. Right, Mrs. Bradley. That would be nice. Black, please. My techs should be right along. Always have time for a cup of coffee."

Martha poured three cups, then sat at the kitchen table, joining the men. "Dr. Goodman, will you be able to tell how long he's been buried in our root cellar? At least I'm presuming it's a man. May be he's why we hear strange ghost-like noises around the house—his spirit rattling to escape," Martha said in a conspiratorial tone, and toothy grin.

"Right, Yes." Goody pushed his wire-rimmed glasses up on his nose, scratched his thatch of silver hair behind his ear, and looked at Martha. "Back in the lab, with the latest forensic techniques, and depending on how much of the skeleton is down there … o'course, the skull will give us some clues. Yes, definitely the age, how long he's been dead ... yes, estimates. A body's long bones, say a leg, will tell us more. If we don't find demineralization of the bones, like an arthritis abnormality, then he's probably under forty years old. If there are signs of significant demineralization then he was probably more than sixty at the time of death."

Martha glanced at her husband. *Demineralization?*

Goodman looked up at the sound of a van, followed by laughter as the techs started unloading their equipment.

"Ah, my men are here. At any rate, Martha, we'll soon know what bones we have. Yes, take everything back to the lab and proceed with the identification—age, sex, height, even race maybe. Thanks for the coffee."

Chapter 7

——

Exeter Gazette
November 18, 1969

BRADLEY HORSE FARM.

Last Sunday, much to the surprise of Arnold and Martha Bradley, a large, bear-cub like stray dog charged into the root cellar when Mr. Bradley opened the cellar's hatch.

The dog started clawing in a frenzy at the earth floor. Mr. Bradley told Dr. Goodman, the city coroner and ME, that it was as if the dog was possessed, dirt flying out behind his hind legs.

The dog unearthed a skull.

Bradley called Chief Roy Saxon to report the finding. Saxon sent out Dr. Goodman, who in turn called in a team to explore the dig, uncovering a complete skeleton. The bones were hauled off to the morgue's laboratory.

As of this writing, nothing more is known about the discovery—who, what, or how the bones happened to be buried in the Bradley root cellar. The one thing the coroner said was that the bones were old, but they have not been examined as yet to determine how old.

Goodman also stated that Martha Bradley told him she felt a whoosh of cold air escape the hatch as the dog dug.

Anyone believe in ghosts?

• • •

"ARNIE? ROY HERE. Did you see the Exeter News this morning?"

"Just opening it, Chief. What am I looking for?"

"Back page, lower left—*Skull Found.* Just wanted to let you know Goody didn't mean to give the reporter the story. She drops by every week to pick up the arrest reports and Goody spilled the beans. He thought it was interesting that a dog found a skeleton in your root cellar."

"Tell Goody he's forgiven, but I want the next pair of aces."

"No way! Have a good day, Arnie."

Arnie could hear the chief chuckling as he disconnected the call.

Martha topped off her husband's coffee mug, sat down picking up the second section of the paper. "What did the chief want?"

"Just a second ... okay, here ... skull article."

Martha scanned the article, handed it back to Arnie. "Did Goody tell the chief anything else ... like *how* old?"

"Nope. So, do you, Martha?"

"Do I what?"

"Believe in ghosts?"

"Hmm, maybe. We certainly have weird noises now and again. Of course, it could just be this old house is settling."

"That must be it." *Yup, she believes in ghosts,* he thought smiling to himself.

Chapter 8

Portsmouth Herald
November 19, 1969

A DOG DUG UP a skull buried in the root cellar of a New Hampshire farmhouse. Dr. Goodman, the local coroner, is running tests to determine the age of the bones.

The farmhouse was built in 1840 so the bones could be upward of a hundred years old.

• • •

Boston Globe
November 20, 1969

ASSOCIATED PRESS
The owners of a New Hampshire horse farm described the actions of a stray, curly haired, mangy dog, as possessed. The farmer and his son had opened the hatch to a root cellar when the mutt darted down into the hole and began digging, uncovering a skull.

Chief Roy Saxon responded to the farmer's call sending out Dr. Goodman, the Medical Examiner, who in turn called in his team. A complete skeleton was uncovered and is now in Goodman's lab for analysis.

When asked why they happened to open the hatch at that time, Mrs. Bradley said she heard noises and asked her husband to check.

There is speculation that the bones may be over a hundred years old. The house has been in the family since their ancestor, Marshall Bradley, built the farmhouse in 1840.

Chapter 9

———

FRANKIE GIOVANNI LOVED scanning the newspaper, the obituaries in particular, checking if any of his old buddies had given up living. His ritual—morning coffee looking out the window of his twenty-first floor condo, and checking the boats tied up in the various Boston marinas below. Clouds had rolled in. A storm was brewing, stirring up the ocean waters. He couldn't smell the salt air through the double-paned windows, but he could imagine it. Satisfied that everything was as it was the night before, he opened the newspaper. An article in the human interest section, just before the obituaries, caught his eye. Reaching for the telephone, he dialed his old friend Vincenzo Scarpetti, sipping the last of his coffee while he waited for his call to be answered.

"Hey, Vincenzo, did you see the story about a skeleton found by a dog in a root cellar of a horse farm? In today's paper."

"Whatta you calling me for?"

"Don't get huffy. I got reasons."

"Such as?"

"Isn't there an old story about your family, Scarpetti? The head of the family disappearing, sudden like, 1880 something? You ask Junior. Your son's always digging around for info on his ancestors."

"I don't pay any attention to him—"

"Yeah? Well, maybe you should. There was a scandal as I recall. The elder Scarpetti moved his mob's operation from New

York. Hid out in New Hampshire. That's how your family happened to settle in New Hampshire. You ask your son. Tony showed me a yellowed newspaper clipping one time."

"A scandal? Disappearing could mean anything. Maybe he wanted to die in peace, a warm place, like Hawaii. Weatherman last night predicted a bad winter this year."

"Wait, I remember. Tony said there was an English guy, like the farmer Bradley in the newspaper, took up with Scarpetti. When Scarpetti disappeared, so did a lotta valuable stuff your family had collected from its operations in New York—jewelry, artwork, and money. Lots of money. Wouldn't it be something if all the stuff was stashed in that farmhouse along with Scarpetti in the root cellar?"

Chapter 10

———

SOMETHING WAS UP.

Jane's parents were chatting nervously as they passed the fried chicken, mashed potatoes and gravy around the dinner table—getting cold outside, looks like snow, car checkup, neighbor's cat.

Kathleen asked her daughter if she wanted another glass of milk with her cherry pie—Jane's favorite.

Jane declined.

"Colin, I think it's time to tell our daughter the big news, the trip we're all taking." A smile flashed across her face, disappearing as quickly as it came, as she cut the pie into wedges, placing them carefully in the center of the small plates, passing the plates of pie to her husband and daughter.

Colin took a bite. "You outdid yourself, Kathleen. The best ever."

"What trip?" Jane asked taking a bite of pie.

Colin looked at his wife, then his daughter. "California, Los Angeles, California. The papers are ready to be signed off on the building my firm is leasing for our western operations. I've been tasked with handling the start up."

"When are you leaving?" Jane held her fork in the air, held her breath.

"Your mother has made all the arrangements to close up the house—electricity, phone, realtor to keep an eye on the house—"

"Where am I going to stay? I have finals coming up. Why can't you stay here, Mother? You both said a move, if there was even going to be a move, wouldn't be until next summer, spring at the earliest."

"Your mother and I thought the change would be good for all of us. Get away from the cold, the snow, give us a chance to look over the area, see where we want to live, see—"

"Where am I staying? Maybe Cilla—"

"Heavens, no, Jane. You're coming with us, of course. We'll all get away from the coming winter go where it's sunny, warm. You'll love—"

"What about school. I'll—"

Kathleen's eyes darted to her husband. "I talked to the principal this afternoon. With your excellent grades, you don't have to take the finals—straight A in all your classes. You'll finish high school ... in LA."

Jane set her fork down on the plate, a cherry sliding off to the side on the white tablecloth. She had never disobeyed her parents. She knew they didn't like Danny. Maybe not so much didn't like him, but that a farmer was not the sort of boy they wanted for their daughter to date. Who knew where it might lead and they didn't want to take any chances.

"When?"

"Your mother has everything arranged, as do I, so ... no point in sticking around. All you have to do is pack your suitcases."

"When?"

"Your father thinks Sunday morning. We'll be in LA for Thanksgiving."

Jane jumped to her feet. "Excuse me," she mumbled over her shoulder as she left the room.

"Aren't you going to finish your pie ... your favorite?" her mother called after her.

"I'm not hungry." Quick steps, then she broke into a run to her bedroom, shutting the door, flinging herself on the flowered bedcover, curling up in a ball around her pillow. The tears began slowly at first, then sobs muffled by the downy pillow.

Her life was over. She was moving away … away from Danny. They had become an item—he walked her to class, carried her books, ate lunch together in the cafeteria. School girls weren't supposed to know about love. School girls were simply feeling a crush, puppy love the teen magazine articles stated.

Well, she loved Danny and now she was leaving him. How was he going to feel? He'd told her he liked her, never known a girl like her. But he never said he loved her, so, maybe he wouldn't care if she left.

Jane fought the blanket throughout the night. Danny had asked her to the movies tomorrow afternoon. She'd have to tell him it was their last date. How could she bear it … the unbearable? She fought the tears. She wouldn't allow herself to be one of those hysterical teenagers. No, she'd be strong. Jane pulled Peter Rabbit under her arm.

Rolling onto her back, she looked into Peter's black button eyes. "I *won't* go, Peter. That's it. Leave, my senior year? I'm not going. Cilla! I'll go see Cilla tomorrow morning … early."

Jane coiled around Peter, her arm tightening around the rabbit. Breathing returning to normal, shutting her eyes, she fell into a fitful sleep.

● ● ●

THE SUN'S RAY SLICED across the beige carpet. Jane kicked her legs from the tangle of sheets and blanket. After a quick shower, she pulled on her jeans, a sweatshirt over a white turtleneck. Hopping out of her room as she tied her sneakers, she breezed through the kitchen.

"Jane, where are you going? You have to pack," her mother said holding the milk bottle mid air.

"I'm going to see Cilla."

"What about breakfast?"

The door swung shut behind her in answer to her mother's question. Pumping the air with her fists, Jane broke into a steady jog. She didn't take the time to call Cilla. Jane knew Cilla slept in on Saturday, so the chances were good she'd be home. Jogging up the driveway to the back door, she punched the doorbell.

A sleepy Cilla pulled the door open, a mug of hot chocolate in her hand, blinking through the screen at Jane.

"Cilla, I have to talk to you."

"Sure, sure, come in. Hot chocolate?"

"Good morning, Jane. You're out early," Cilla's mom said buttering a piece of whole wheat toast.

"Cilla, can we go to your room?" Jane whispered.

"Sure, sure." Cilla led the way, her pink kitten slippers shuffling down the hall.

Cilla climbed up on her bed, leaned back against the headboard, and took a sip of cocoa.

"Cilla, I'm in a jam."

Cilla eyed her friend. "Can't be a failing grade, you—"

"My parents are dragging me to California … tomorrow."

"Wow, that's fun. Thanksgiving in warm, sunny California."

"You don't understand. We're moving … for good."

"Oh my God."

"Cilla, can I live with you … till June … till we graduate? I'll work. Pay room and board—"

"Jane, I don't know." Cilla set her empty mug down on the bedside table. "Wait here. Let me see what my mom says."

Jane let out a sigh. Cilla seemed open to the idea, she thought. Maybe there's a chance.

She looked around the room. She had slept over a few times but had only hung out in Cilla's bedroom and the kitchen. Both rooms were smaller than she remembered. *Maybe they didn't have another bedroom … a small bed could fit in here … a cot.*

Cilla strolled back into her bedroom, hitched up on the bed, crossed her legs Indian style. "My mom said she had to talk to Dad. If he said it was okay, she said she was okay, but she had to call your mom first which she did, right then. I heard her end of the conversation. There is *no* discussion. Your folks are taking you with them. It would have been fun, Jane."

Jane stared into Cilla's eyes. There was no hope.

"I'm so sorry, Jane."

"Okay. It's okay, Cilla. Thanks for trying. I have to run," Jane said, her feet swinging off the bed.

Both girls stood, hesitated, then hugged.

"Bye, Cilla."

"Bye, Jane."

Chapter 11

———

JANE STOOD ON THE curb waiting for Danny. Her fists clenched as she stepped back, paced, wishing the sidewalk would open, swallow her up, the skirt of her navy-blue dress flipping with each turn in her step.

She heard the truck round the corner pulling up in front of her house. Not giving Danny a chance to help, she jerked the truck door open, and with two hops on the step, she was inside. Swinging the door shut, snapping the seatbelt in place, she fixed her eyes straight ahead, hands clasped together tightly in her lap.

Danny laid his hand over hers, his mouth opened then closed as he slowly rolled the truck away from the curb and down the street. Turning the corner, he pulled to a stop in front of a yellow clapboard house.

Twisting to face Jane, he reached for her hand again.

Without looking, Jane's fingers fastened around his.

"Janie, did I do something wrong?"

"I'm moving ... far away."

Danny's brows scrunched together. "Why?"

"My father is being sent by his company to set up a new division."

"Where?"

"Los Angeles."

Jane turned to face him. She couldn't help herself—a tear slipped over her lid dropping onto Danny's fingers.

"When?"

"In the morning ... a realtor is taking care of the house ... I have to pack my clothes today." She searched his eyes staring back at her, trying to comprehend what she was saying.

Danny lifted her knuckles to his lips. "Do you want to go to the movie? It starts—"

"Do you?"

"Not really."

"Me either."

"Let's head out to The Birches. Have lunch."

"That's kind of expensive. You don't really—"

"Have you been there?"

"Once. My parents took me on one of their anniversaries. Out in the country. Very pretty. Nestled in a grove of birch trees on a lake."

"That's the place."

Danny popped the glove compartment, snatched a tissue wiping a teardrop away from each of Jane's eyes. "There, pretty as ever."

Jane sucked in a breath of air. "Thanks," she whispered.

Danny put the truck in gear and headed out of town. He kept glancing at her, his face somber, sadness filling his eyes, worry lines creasing his brow.

At The Birches, they both ordered a chicken sandwich and a coke. Conversation was light, mostly about Suzy's antics with the mutt. His mom had relented, giving in to Suzy's sad eyes, and let the mutt stay for a while especially because of the chance reporter stopping by wanting to take a picture of the curly-haired, bear-cub of a dog who dug up a skull. For lack of a better name, the mutt became known as Dog with a capital D.

Danny paid the waitress, laid down a tip on the table, and picked up Jane's hand absentmindedly stroking her fingers.

"We'll write to each other, Janie. I want to hear about everything you're doing ... even if you meet a tall, blonde surfer dude."

"That's not going to happen. And I want to know about all the basketball games … and your band … and if you get tired of writing—"

"That's never going to happen. This is so sudden." He paused looking out at the lake. "I have an idea."

"What's that?"

"Come on, let's go." He took her hand, his dark brown eyes smiling over a spreading grin.

"Where are we going?"

"The drugstore. The picture booth. We're going to take our pictures, not that I need one to remember your pretty red curls or those killer green eyes, but I want one to carry with me. OK?"

"That's a great idea."

• • •

LEAVING THE DRUGSTORE, several pictures in hand—Jane had insisted on one with only Danny, and he insisted on one with only her, one he could talk to—he drove slowly to her house. Parking the truck at the curb, he turned to Jane, again pressing her hand to his lips. "Sit tight. I'll get your door."

Jane didn't know what it was like to faint, but she felt her chest tighten as she gulped for air.

The truck door opened, Danny reached up taking her hand. His fingers gripping her fingers, they strolled up the walk, up the steps to the front porch.

Danny turned Jane into his arms holding her to him. He leaned back, kissed her lips. He had kissed her before, but this was different—urgent, sad, lost. "I love you, Janie."

"I love you too, Danny. What are we going to do?"

"I don't know."

Chapter 12

JANE SHUT HER BEDROOM DOOR, picked up her notebook and sat cross legged on her bed. In the light of the bedside lamp, she opened the notebook to a blank page, the page after her English assignment. With a sigh, pushing up the sleeves on her pale blue pajamas, she began to write a letter to Danny.

• • •

December 2
Dear Danny,
The sun is shining. It's always shining in LA.

My first day at West High was nerve-racking, but by the end of the day I felt I could handle it. The teachers were very kind and, one-on-one, showed me the class assignments. I brought some of my past assignments with me so I could show each teacher what I was studying when I left New Hampshire, especially important for math and English. I think they were surprised. We'll see how I do on the first round of tests.

The kids are friendly for the most part, other than everyone is blonde from the sun or a bottle. I stick out with my red curls. That's another thing. All the girls have long, long blonde hair, straight blonde hair.

My parents rented what is called a bungalow three blocks from the beach. They are pulling out all stops to convince me I should love LA.

So, what's not to like?

The number one not-to-like is that you're not here. The second not-to-like I AM here. Either way ... I hate it!

I miss Bradley Horse Farm—your parents, Sir Charles, and Suzy.

But, Danny, I miss you most of all. Did you mean what you said when you kissed me goodbye on the porch? Did you mean it when you said you love me? I meant my reply.

I love you too, Daniel Bradley.

Janie

Chapter 13

———

HE HAD TO TALK to his dad. Burning in his two front pockets were Janie's picture in one and her letter in the other. Danny dug his toe in the dirt path, stuffed his hands in his back pockets and headed down to the horse barn.

Arnie was vigorously brushing Sir Charles when his son entered the barn and slumped on top of a hay bale.

"What's up, son. You look like you lost your best friend. No word from Janie yet?"

Without answering, Danny pulled out Janie's letter, handing it to his dad. Arnie read the letter penned three-thousand miles away. Folding the sheet on its original creases, he handed the letter back to his son, and resumed brushing the withers of the big horse.

Danny leaned back against the rough pine boards of the stall. "When did you know mom was the one?"

Arnie thought a minute. He sat on a hay bale next to Danny, carefully selected a piece of straw and began chewing the end. "From the minute I saw her. Seems to me you have a lot bouncing around in that head of yours."

"What should I do?"

"Do you love her?"

"Yes. Since she left, all the fun, excitement I once had leading the team—football field, boards of the basketball court—are gone. I see her everywhere on the farm. Everyplace we hiked, her questions—always wanting to know why we did something a certain way, questioning mom at dinner about the origin of copper penny carrots. Full of curiosity. I miss her more each day, and I'm worried I might lose her."

"Seems to me you've answered your own question ... if she's the one. Only thing remaining is what do you do about it?"

"Her parents will never let her come back. I don't think they approve of me."

"What makes you think that?"

"The way they whisked her away. Never gave her a chance to think. They saw an opportunity to break us up and acted."

"How old is Jane?"

"Seventeen. Turns eighteen on April 15. We joked about it being tax day and that it was no wonder she was so good at math."

"I see. You both graduate next June. Seems to me there's nothing you can do until you both graduate. Then you both are of an age when you can make your own decisions. But, if her parents feel as you say about you, which I find very hard to believe—of course, I guess I'm biased—then a relationship with her is going to be a struggle. They don't really know you. Anyway the two of you can decide if you want to be together, if you want to marry."

"You and Mom—you were nineteen ... she was eighteen?"

"That's right."

"Seems like that turned out pretty good."

"Yes, it did."

"There's another thing."

"What's that, son?"

"You know I'm eligible for the draft?"

"It's a lottery, Danny, you may not—"

"I know. But I wanted to tell you, if I receive the notice, I won't try to get out of it and I'll ask you and Mom not to intervene."

"You want to join the fight like your grandfather. Mason Bradley fought in WWI. Almost died of his wounds but he made it back to the farm. He thought he was indestructible after that, took up horse racing and then cars. Died at the age of fifty. Heart attack."

"I've read some of his journals. Found them in the attic—fascinating, the places he saw."

"Yup. Lots of thoughts bouncing around in your head. Now, let's finish up with Sir Charles. He's getting impatient to be let out for a run in the fields."

Chapter 14

———

DECEMBER 15

Dear Janie,

Yes, I love you!

I asked my dad when he knew Mom was the one. He said the minute he saw her for the first time.

That's exactly how I felt when I sat next to you in the school library and asked if you would help me with math. You looked up at me with those beautiful green eyes and I was a goner.

You asked me, what we are we going to do three-thousand miles apart.

The holidays are coming, and then the new year will start. As I see it, the best thing we can do is buckle down with our classes. Well, you not so much, but without my personal tutor I definitely have to buckle down.

Hopefully, the time will pass quickly, although I doubt it will. June seems a long way away but we have to graduate … then … well, then we'll see. I've started saving to buy you a plane ticket. ONE WAY. How does that sound?

My dad said if we truly love each other, we'll find a way. But he thinks we have to wait until after we graduate.

I love you,

Danny

Chapter 15

_____

DECEMBER 24

Dear Danny,

It's Christmas Eve—no snowflakes, no icy breeze, only more sun and sand. My parents love it, keep saying how great it is they don't have to shovel snow to get out of the driveway.

Merry Christmas.

The new year is around the corner. I bought a new calendar yesterday. Graduation at West High is scheduled for Saturday, June second. I drew a big red circle around the square. That makes it five months and nine days to the BIG day.

I like your idea of my flying to New Hampshire on June third if we can swing it. I wouldn't think of asking you to pay for my whole ticket. I plan to get a part-time job. We have to be pragmatic about this. We'll pool our money. I'm sure we can make it.

Graduation, June, seem years away. But each day I'll put a big X in the square on my calendar.

We have a plan. I can almost smile thinking about it.

Miss you terribly.

Love you,

Janie

PS: my calendar has an enormous black horse on the front. Looks like Sir Charles.

Chapter 16

———

JANE RAN INTO THE DRUGSTORE, plunked down a five dollar bill in front of the cashier and asked her for twenty quarters in exchange. She had an important phone call to make and she certainly didn't want to run out of money.

The cashier counted out the quarters making up the last dollar with dimes. She smiled at the pretty redhead, her curls and eyes sparking in excitement.

Jane thanked the women then stepped to the phone booth in the back corner of the store. Rocking back and forth in her white sneakers, Jane waited for the man to finish his call. He finally hung up, fingered the change from the slot, and left.

Jane stepped into the booth, settled her purse on the floor, stacked the coins on the shelf under the phone, and dialed the number she knew by heart.

"Happy New Year," the male voice said in greeting.

"Hi, Mr. Bradley. This is Jane O'Neill, Danny's—"

"Jane! What a nice surprise. And it's Arnie. Have you forgotten already? It hasn't been that long has it?"

"No, Arnie, I didn't forget. It's well ... is Danny there?"

"He is. Waving a hand in front of my face when I said your name. Happy New Year, dear."

"And, to you ... and Danny's mom."

"Janie, is it really you. Where are you?"

Jane giggled. Oh, it was so wonderful to hear Danny's voice. "I'm in a phone booth, in a drugstore, I had to call. You aren't going to believe this. I had a serious talk with my parents last night. I told them I wanted to return to New Hampshire for the final months of school after spring break. It was only fair that they let me graduate from high school with my friends. I told them I had done everything they asked of me, and now I wanted this more than anything, so much so I threatened to hitchhike if necessary."

"Wow! Tell me, tell me, what did they say?"

"I think they were tired of seeing my long face. THEY SAID YES! DANNY, THEY SAID YES! It's my birthday present. My mother and I are flying home on April fifth. CAN YOU BELIEVE IT? Wait, wait, I have to feed the phone."

"Very pragmatic of you ... having the coins ready."

"What?"

"Your last letter. You said we have to be pragmatic. I agreed after I looked up the word, of course."

Jane giggled, pushing the last of the coins in the slot. "Okay, we're good."

"Janie, this is the best news ever. Let me know if I can pick you and your mother up at the airport. Wow, we can start making plans for graduation, the parties, the dance ... Janie ...

"What?"

"No more being apart."

"I agree. I love you, Daniel Bradley."

"And, I love you, Janie O'Neill."

Part II
Chapter 17

High School Graduation, 1970

WITH LAUGHTER, TEARS, and promises to keep in touch, the high school graduates held their partners close. Dancing at their last high school event, couples paused now and again to exchange hugs, guys punching another guy's arm, friends kissing cheeks.

Yearbooks were distributed the week before, passed between students for autographs, simple words of good luck, or funny comments about jokes shared between them over the years.

Grades were received, addresses traded.

The frenzy of activity was winding down. The graduation ceremony was scheduled to take place the day after tomorrow. The day graduates would swing the tassel on their mortarboard from the right side to the left. The day the graduates would accept their diploma, march off the stage to begin the next phase of their life's journey.

But tonight was personal. Students shedding the last vestiges of the bond they had shared over the years, some from the time they attended grade school together.

Jane took Danny's breath away when he picked her up. She had splurged on a pale lavender, sleeveless chiffon dress. The fabric floated over lavender silk, the hem flirting with her knees when they danced. Beveled gold hoops, her only jewelry, glistened next to her red curls. Holding her close in a slow dance, Danny breathed in the scent of lavender behind her ears. A trick she picked up from a California girly magazine.

Cilla, her current beau in tow, tapped Danny on the shoulder. "Hey, you guys, we're going to the church hall after the dance. They're putting on a midnight feast for us grads. Are you going? Please say yes."

Danny surprised Jane. They had talked about going to the church party, that it would be fun. With graduation two days later, two more days until they said goodbye to their youth, to their friends who would scatter the minute the graduation ceremony was over. Danny, his arm tight around Jane's waist, told Cilla that they weren't going.

Cilla pouted. "What's the matter? You're the captain of the football team. Basketball team. All of a sudden you're too good for us?" Gripping her partner's hand, Cilla ushered him away from Danny and a bewildered Jane.

Danny grasped Jane's hand. "Let's get out of here." He marched her away from the band, away from the gaiety of the graduates, out the door into the humid night. Clouds had formed covering the moon one second, the next second the beams of light found a hole lighting up the countryside again.

Jane didn't question Danny's strange behavior. She had learned that he would eventually tell her what was bothering him. She only had to be patient.

"Janie, I'm sorry. We can go back if you want."

Jane faced the boy she loved, placed her palms on his chest, searching his face for an answer.

"It's just I have something planned. I want to show you something back at the farm, just you and me."

On tiptoe, she kissed him, took his hand, nodding to him to lead the way.

She didn't know that since her call on New Year's Day, telling Danny that she was coming home, he began planning a special moment. The lake on the edge of the farm, that was to be the place. He'd found an old carriage seat made of hickory in one of the barns. He confided to his dad what he was going to do, asked if he could use one of the stalls to set up a workbench. Nothing fancy, a small space where he could refinish the bench.

Yesterday, he had positioned the carriage seat on the shores of the lake beneath a tall birch tree, its white bark glistening in the sunlight. Checking the weather report, the heavens were supposed to cooperate. A clear sky was in the forecast, perhaps a few cloud skiffs, but no rain. The moon and stars would be the back drop for the big moment.

● ● ●

THE RED TRUCK BUMPED along the dirt road, passed the barns, coming to a stop by a path. A diamond engagement ring, a solitaire, burned in Danny's jacket pocket. The purchase took almost all the money he earned for working on the farm — pennies, loose change, dollar bills saved in a jar since Christmas. It wasn't a big diamond but neither was it a chip. Someday he planned to give her a bigger one. Maybe for a birthday present, or an anniversary. Yeah, an anniversary.

"The spot I picked out on the lake is a few yards away … what about your feet? Those heels look pretty delicate. I have a clean pair of socks. Want to put them on?"

Jane looked out the open window. Her gold strappy heels were not designed for walking on a dirt path. "Sure, but don't laugh. Socks are going to spoil my—"

"Believe me, nothing is going to take away from how beautiful you look."

Reaching behind his seat, he came up with a pair of white crew socks. Running around to open her door, she flipped off the gold heels. Bending down Danny slipped the crew socks over her pink painted toes.

They walked hand in hand down the path to the lake. Crickets stopped their chirping as they approached, resuming the rubbing of their wings as they passed.

At the edge of the lake Danny turned her to him, softly kissed her eager lips. "I love you, Janie. I want to be with you for life. I want children with you."

Her breath caught in her throat. Did she hear him right? She loved him more than life itself as he again professed his love for her. "Danny, I love you too," she whispered.

Danny sat on the carriage seat, gently pulling her down on his lap. In the crisp moonlight laced with stars, he reached into his shirt pocket and held the diamond up to her.

"Danny, a ring, a diamond ring ... does this mean ...

"We talked about getting married next Christmas, but ...

"What's the matter, Daniel Bradley? Are you suddenly too shy to ask me to marry you?"

"I won the lottery." He paused. The words stuck in his throat.

"What? You won this beautiful ring in a lottery?"

"I've been drafted. I have to report in three days for a physical and psychological exam in Portsmouth. If I pass, I'll be inducted into the Army the same day. I may or may not be able to come home for a few days before reporting to boot camp."

Jane held up her left hand, wiggling her ring finger.

"Are you sure, Janie?"

"I have never been so sure of anything in my life. I love you, Daniel Bradley. Now, please put that ring on my finger."

Chapter 18

———

THE AROMA OF blueberry pancakes and fresh coffee curled under Jane's bedroom door. Snuggling deeper under the sheet blanket, she drew her hand out catching the beam of sunshine. The diamond was brilliant sending rainbows to her eyes and a smile to her lips. Kissing the stone, she felt its heat in her belly, heat replaced with the stab of a clenched knot. Danny's words rang in her ears—drafted, leaving in a few days.

Springing from the covers, she raised her head, stiffened her spine as she held her hand up. She was engaged! It was a bright beautiful day and she would let nothing spoil it.

Not even her parents.

Suddenly, filled with apprehension, she raised her hand again, twitching her fingers in the sunlight. Taking a deep breath, turning her head to the mirror over her dresser, she gazed at her reflection.

Today she was a woman, a woman engaged to be married. Married at Christmas time. A beautiful, magical holiday. Danny said he thought he could get a few days leave. He was sure of it, as he slipped the ring on her finger.

Jane smiled at the woman looking back at her, a determined face, eyes reflecting resolve. Danny was picking her up at noon, driving her back to the farm to tell his parents the news—he had asked Jane to be his wife.

Jane pulled a pair of denim shorts from the dresser. Shook her head. Today she must wear a dress, show the world that she is a woman. She could wear the shorts tomorrow, but not today. Two dresses hung in the closet. One for Sunday church, the second was new. An apple green sheath that said there's a woman inside. The green was spectacular against her red hair, bringing out her emerald eyes. She was definitely going to make an impression, an impression on Danny, showing him that this woman loved him. Second, an impression on their parents—she had morphed from a girl into a woman overnight.

Pushing her sneakers to the side, she slipped her feet into a pair of white flats, polished the day before to wear with her graduation robe. She fastened the pair of gold hoops in her ears that she wore to the dance last night.

She was ready.

She turned, walked down the stairs, each step faster than the last, her left hand held behind her.

Her father had flown home two days ago to escort Kathleen to their daughter's graduation. He was reading the newspaper as Jane entered the kitchen.

"Good morning, Jane. Have a seat. Your father has some news. I'll pour your milk, French toast coming up."

"I'd like a cup of coffee this morning, Mother."

"Since when did you start drinking coffee?" her mother asked.

"It smells particularly nice this morning. I have some news too. You first, Father."

"I put in an offer on a house, similar to the house your mother and I looked at, in the neighborhood we liked."

"It's lovely, Jane. Your father has pictures. I'm sure you'll like it." Kathleen's eyes darted to her husband's. "It's not too far from the University of California."

"What your mother is saying is that the owner of the house accepted our offer. We spoke to the realtor who was looking after this house until we were sure we were going to sell. We're putting everything in her hands."

"It's a permanent move, Jane," her mother said adding a fresh stack of French toast to the platter. She checked the syrup pitcher. Set it back on the table.

"I'm not going!"

Her father stopped chewing a bite of pancake, wiped his mouth with a napkin, looked at his wife, then at his daughter.

"Danny asked me to marry him." Jane picked up the mug of coffee curling her hand so the diamond faced her father.

Kathleen fixed her eyes on her daughter. "The movers are coming on Monday. It may seem sudden but you knew your father only came for your graduation, that we would be returning with him. After the movers load the few items we're taking, we'll spend the night at the Exeter Inn, leave the next morning for Los Angeles."

"So, Jane," her father began, "you have three days to come to your senses."

"I don't need three days. I don't need one day or one hour. Danny has been drafted. He leaves in three days. I'll be spending most of my time with him."

"And then what, Jane?"

She looked at her father. His voice was stern. His eyes icy.

Her mother cut in. "You understand that Danny is a farm boy. You are a city girl. Hardly a match made in heaven. You know nothing of farming. Labor, that's what it is—hard labor. In the service? For how long?"

"Two years."

"Two years. Where will you live? You have no money?"

"I'll get a job. Maybe stay with Cilla."

"Two years? I hardly think Cilla's parents will want a free loader for two years."

"We're going to be married at Christmas time."

"Which Christmas? Next, or a year from?" her father asked, sliding his empty coffee mug to his wife.

"This Christmas."

Hearing Danny close his truck door, Jane looked up, looked out through the screen door. He had a big smile on his face seeing her appear, holding the screen open for him.

Leaning in, giving her a peck on the cheek, he whispered in her ear. "You look beautiful. I love you."

She whispered back, "I told them. Love you, too."

The couple turned to face her parents.

"Sorry to hear you were drafted, Danny," Mr. O'Neill said.

"Don't feel sorry, sir. I'm proud to serve my country. I'll fight for a life with Jane. I love your daughter. It will hurt like the devil to leave her, but knowing she is waiting for me ... well, I hope the time passes quickly."

"Certainly not a very nice thing to do ... something a teenager would do ... ask a girl to marry him, leave, so she has to put her life on hold," her father said. "Very inconsiderate I'd say. Just what kind of a life are you offering our daughter? I'll tell you—a hard life on a farm."

"Father, Danny and I had talked about getting married months ago. He bought the ring before he knew his draft number was called. He let me make the decision ...whether I wanted to wait until he came home from serving our country before I wore his ring. I asked him to put the ring on my finger *now*."

Chapter 19

———

JANE KISSED THE BRILLIANT stone on her left hand, turned away from her mother and father, and marched defiantly out the screen door.

Danny looked at Mr. O'Neill, then Mrs. O'Neill. "I'm sorry, sir, Mrs. O'Neill."

"You should have asked us, Daniel," Mr. O'Neill said, He stood with his feet apart, hands on his hips, staring the boy down.

Danny shook his head in disbelief, followed Jane out into the hot, humid, summer air. Giving Jane a hand up into the truck, he buckled her seatbelt. Taking his place behind the wheel, he backed out of the driveway and headed to the farm to tell his parents of their engagement.

Staring at the fields sliding by the truck window, Jane felt Danny's warm fingers curl around her hand. Turning to him, her eyes scanned his face. "I love you, Danny. Whatever your parents say, I love you."

Danny glanced sideways at his fiancé. "And, Miss Jane O'Neill, I love you. I'm proud to present you to my parents as the girl I've chosen to be my wife. I'm going to get my camera before I bring you back home. I want a picture of you in that green dress. I'll carry it with me for luck. Now, put a smile on your face." His voice was soft, gentle, but unwavering.

Jane leaned against the seatbelt, her lips grazing his cheek, then settled back looking out the windshield. "My parents are selling the house."

"When?"

"They said they waited to tell me until after graduation. I guess I forced them to say something this morning. They've known for several weeks. The movers are coming Monday and they plan to leave for California the next day. They laid down an ultimatum. I have to go with them."

"Wow," Danny said blowing out a breath of air.

"I'm not going. I'm staying right here, waiting for you. I'll ask Cilla if I can stay with her family. I'll think of something."

Danny pulled to the side of the road, leaving the motor idling. "Janie, *we'll* think of something. You are not alone. We'll work it out ... together."

"You mean it, Danny? I thought you might want your ring back."

"Janie, don't ever doubt my love for you ... ever. Got that?"

Jane's green eyes locked on his big black ones. "Got it." Her voice was strong, her heart pounding. "And don't you ever doubt mine!"

"Okay."

"Now, let's go to the farm, tell your parents our big news."

Danny put his hands on her cheeks raising her lips to his. Then, squaring his body behind the wheel, he pulled away from the grassy shoulder alongside the street.

The red truck raced down the country road, the boy holding the girl's hand, the ring warm on her finger, binding their hearts together.

● ● ●

DANNY'S DAD SPOTTED the truck pulling off the road, driving up to the house. A smile spread across his face, his eyes twinkling. He watched his son help the pretty Irish beauty wearing an apple green dress out of the truck.

His son, the romantic. But … where did the skinny little boy go? When? He's taller than I am. And that chest, the shoulders … heck those biceps.

Arnie knew the boy had popped the question. He could see it in the care he took helping her out of the truck, as if she was a princess, his princess. Arnie remembered the day, years ago, when he had the same look in his eyes asking his mother to marry him. The boy seemed taller, older, as hand in hand the couple approached him.

"Hi, Dad, where's Mom? Jane and I have something to tell you."

"In the kitchen, son. Good morning, Jane. Lovely day, don't you think?"

"Yes, sir. A very lovely day." Jane smiled.

Arnie smiled to himself as he led the way into the house. Darned if Jane didn't look taller, older, same as his son. They'd need that confidence because Martha was not going to like what their son was going to say. No, she wasn't going to like it one bit.

Martha pushed the button on the coffeemaker. She had heard the familiar rattle of Danny's truck engine. She glanced at her son as he entered the kitchen holding Jane's hand as if she might float away. The ring on the girl's finger flashed in Martha's eyes.

"Mom, Dad, I've asked Janie to marry me and—"

"I said, yes." Jane broke in, a broad smile across her face, squeezing Danny's hand as her eyes sought his.

Arnie stepped into the electric silence, blunting the shock waves. "Well, I think that's wonderful. Congratulations." He wrapped Jane in a warm hug, shook his son's hand. "Martha, aren't you going to congratulate your son and daughter-in-law to be?"

Martha's face was not one of happiness but of pain. "I see you've both made up your minds, but Jane you know nothing of farm life. Or, Danny, are you planning to leave the farm? Live someplace else?"

"Mom, of course, I'm not leaving the farm." Danny quickly stepped to his mother, hugged her tight. "The farm is part of me. I would never leave here."

"What about you Jane? You're a city girl."

Danny relinquished the hold on his mom as she put her question to Jane.

"Mrs. Bradley, I love Danny. Where he is, I will be ... right beside him."

"You know that Danny will be inducted into the Army in a few days, leaving here for two years."

"Martha, of course, she knows. With graduation tomorrow, how about inviting Jane over for dinner after the ceremony? A celebration."

Martha looked at her husband. "Of course. Celebrate the fact that our son is leaving for war?"

"Martha, you know that's not what I meant. When are you two planning to be married?"

"We thought a holiday wedding. No date yet, but sometime over Christmas," Danny said. *Surely the worst is over*, he thought. "Dad, you and I could hitch up Sir Charles to the sleigh, take us all to the church. If no snow, then a wagon decorated with lights— battery lit to bring the sleigh to life. A beautiful beginning of a new life as husband and wife."

"What Christmas? The one coming, the next, the next after that?"

"This coming Christmas, Mom. I'm sure I'll get leave ... or around that time. Whenever. We'll make it our own Christmas. Right, Janie." Danny lifted Jane in the air, twirling her around. "Right?"

"Right," she said giggling. "Danny, I have to call Cilla. Is there a phone, where I can talk privately?" Jane whispered.

"Yes, in Mom's office. Come on, I'll show you."

• • •

"HI, CILLA. IT'S ME, JANE."

"Why are you whispering?" Cilla asked.

"Danny asked me to marry him last night … we're engaged."

"You what?"

"I have a huge favor to ask. I'll explain later, but can I sleep over at your house for a couple of nights? We can gossip, trade stories about graduation … and my engagement. Do you think your mom would mind?"

"Of course she won't mind. Sounds fun. Tonight?"

"No, Monday night. Danny leaves Monday morning for Portsmouth … on the bus. He's been drafted. I'll explain everything when I see you at graduation tomorrow. But mainly the induction process starts in Portsmouth. Then he comes home for one or two weeks, hopefully, before leaving for boot camp. Very complicated."

"I get it … your mother and father aren't happy so you want to get away. Right?"

"Sort of. You're sure it will be okay with your mom? The last time—"

"I'll confirm this afternoon."

"Okay."

As Jane placed the receiver in the cradle, Danny came up behind her, put his arms around her, pulling her tight to him. "I take it Cilla said yes?"

"Yes she did, but she still has to confirm it with her mom. At least I have a place to stay for a few nights. I didn't ask for more … testing the water I guess. Maybe I can find a room. You still think you'll be home for a few days between going to Portsmouth and reporting to boot camp?"

"That's what I was told. I was also told to expect the unexpected. Write down Cilla's number so I have a way to call you. Of course I'll be in touch with mom and dad, you can call here. I'll ask them to help us stay in touch … at least for a few days, maybe a week, then I have to report. It sounds confusing." Danny planted a kiss on each of her cheeks. "We'll take one day at a time. It will all work out. You'll see. And tomorrow, Janie O'Neill, we have a graduation to attend. Our graduation."

Chapter 20

———

GRADUATION WAS BITTERSWEET—saying goodbye to their friends. Danny received two letters for his sweater—one for football, one for basketball. Students jumped to their feet cheering, giving the team captain a standing ovation. Jane was awarded a thousand dollar scholarship to the college of her choice. Surprised at the announcement, her brows shot up as she quickly stepped to the stage to accept the envelope.

College!

She had forgotten about continuing her education, something her parents had insisted she do. With the exhilaration of being home, being with Danny, maybe she didn't forget, just tuned her parents out. And then there was the For Sale sign mounted in the front lawn announcing the sale of the home she grew up in. But the biggest event, sending her mind and body whirling, was her engagement and then the bad part—Danny was leaving.

Her parents escorted their daughter to the graduation ceremony expecting to go out for dinner afterward. Jane didn't want to be disrespectful, but she also didn't want a lecture, or worse, continued insistence she return to California with them. She thanked them, but said she was meeting Danny and friends after the ceremony ... but she would be home later to pack what she wanted to keep. She told them on the way to the graduation that she was staying with Cilla, and she hoped there was room in her parent's garage to store what little she was keeping. She would be staying with Cilla starting Monday night.

• • •

THE CELEBRATION DINNER at the farm was pleasant but strained. No one mentioned their engagement or Danny's leaving in the morning.

Danny wanted to hold back time, every minute before he had to board the bus Monday morning to the Army induction center in Portsmouth. His fingers tapped the steering wheel as his truck cruised slowly down the road from the farm to Jane's house.

Jane leaned close, Danny's arm around her shoulders. "Your parents aren't happy about our engagement," she murmured with a sigh.

"No, but they'll come around. Dad understood. Are Cilla's parents still okay with your staying with her for a few days?"

"Yes, they really came around. But I have to look for a room, or something, after you catch your bus. What time does it leave again? I keep forgetting."

"10:05. I'll come by for you at eight. We can have breakfast at the café by the bus station. Also, I've been thinking. If you still want to stay ... not leave with your parents—"

"Danny, I'm not leaving. I won't change my mind."

"Your parents will try to persuade you, up to the last minute. I'm just saying, if you don't change your mind, you can finish packing your things with the empty boxes I put in the back of the truck. I asked Dad this morning if you can store the boxes in the cow barn. He said yes."

"Oh, Danny, that is so nice. Better than Cilla's garage. I was going to have to move everything again to find permanent storage someplace."

"Did you take Driver's Ed last year?"

"You know I did," she said with a laugh, punching him in the arm. "The instructor said I was a model student."

"Do you have your driver's license?"

"Yes, have it right here in my wallet," she said patting her little shoulder purse.

"Okay, because I'm going to leave my truck with you when I catch the bus. Then you'll—"

"Danny, do you mean it? That will help beyond ... beyond ... I didn't know what I was going to do."

"Sure, I mean it. You have to have a way to come and go in town ... looking for a job, a room, getting to Cilla's. When I come by for you in the morning we'll put your boxes in the truck. After I catch the bus will you go back home while the movers are there, say goodbye to your mother and father?"

"Yes. I was going to ask you to put my bicycle in the truck. I'd still like to have it."

"Sounds good."

Danny turned into the O'Neill driveway and parked. The truck windows were down allowing the soft summer breeze to circulate the cab. Danny turned to Jane, took her hand, ran his thumb over the engagement ring he had slipped on her finger a few days ago. He looked up into her eyes. "Janie, I love you. In case I don't get home before going to boot camp, I want you to know that I'll write ... as often as I can. I'll send my letters in care of my folks, at the farm, until you have an address."

"And I'll write to you."

Danny squirmed to get his hand in his pants pocket retrieving his wallet. "Here's a hundred dollars—"

"No, no, Danny. You don't have to give me any money."

"How much do you have, right now?"

"I have two dollars in my purse, and eighty-five in the bottom drawer of my jewelry box. I've been saving."

"That's good. You take this. It will help tide you over until you get a job, a room. Janie, I don't see how you're going to manage. If your folks weren't moving—"

"Danny, I'll make it. I'm sure I'll have a job before your bus arrives in Portsmouth. I've already talked to Buddy at the soda fountain across from the theater. He said he'd put in a good word for me with the manager. The job won't be much, but it will be a start. I also called the University of New Hampshire, the Extension Division, about taking a course."

"I don't know how you can swing all that but, knowing you, I'm sure you'll find a way. You're a strong girl."

"Make that a strong woman. A woman who loves you very much. It's been quite a few days—both sets of parents know we're engaged and *we* have a plan for our future."

"Don't forget the biggest part of that plan. We're getting married during the Christmas holidays."

"Oh, I've been dreaming of that since you gave me this beautiful ring. I'm not letting you wiggle out of that." Jane accepted his kiss and then leaned back. "I have to go in. Let's take the boxes out of the truck, put them on the grass. I'll come out for them when I'm ready to pack. I may even ask the movers tomorrow to put my dresser and bed in the truck. Do you think there will be room in the cow barn?"

"You bet, and if not, there are other sheds. I'm going to miss you, Janie. I wish I wasn't leaving you with all this."

● ● ●

KATHLEEN POKED HER HEAD in her daughter's room. Jane was sitting on the floor applying tape sealing the last box. "I wish you'd change your mind, Jane."

"Danny is picking me up in the morning, taking me to breakfast before he takes the bus. He's leaving me his truck while he's away."

"So, you have everything figured out do you. Just so you know, your father and I are going to leave as soon as the movers finish tomorrow. We'll drive for a few hours. See if we can make it to Albany. I hope you come to your senses in the morning and come with us."

"I'm taking my bed and dresser if that's all right."

"Take whatever you like. Just remember when the movers finish loading the van that's it. When you decide you've made a mistake, call us. I've given you the office number at the new facility. We want you to live with us, go to school in California. You love the beach. Just call us. We'll send you money for a train ticket. But you're on your own if you insist on marrying Daniel Bradley. Farm life is not—"

"I know. I know. Farm life is not for a city girl."

Chapter 21

———

HUSHED CONVERSATION, clinking of knives and forks cutting French toast, pancakes, sausage, swirled around the café. The waitress, an order pad peeking out of the pocket of her white bib apron, circled the customers with a coffee pot, stopping here and there to top off half-empty mugs. Patrons, not too eager to start their work week, grabbed an extra jolt of caffeine.

Sitting in a red leatherette booth, Jane and Danny quietly finished their coffee, Danny's arm extended across the table holding tight to Jane's hand.

"How's your coffee?" Danny asked. "Maybe a little cream? Believe me you'll get to like it. I have a big mug every morning before I start my chores. Clears the fog." He smiled.

Jane put on a brave face, sucked in a breath of air, stiffened her spine. She smoothed her green T-shirt over her tan capris. "I like it black and, yes, I feel the fog lifting." Her smile was genuine below her slightly furrowed brows and sad eyes. She felt for the tissue in her pocket ... just in case. A green ribbon, the same green as her T-shirt, held her springy red curls back in a short ponytail.

"We'd better get going. Mom and Dad are waiting for us at the station." Danny put a few coins down for the tip. "I'll pay at the cash register, then, Janie, I want you to drive. I know it's only a block but you have to drive the truck so I know you're okay. It's an automatic. You'll be fine, but I want you to be comfortable."

He handed her the keys hanging from a new brass ring and chain. Closing her fist around the keys, he kissed her hand then walked to the register. A few words with the waitress about the nice sunny day, and Jane slipped out the door Danny was holding open for her.

Danny stood back giving her room to open the truck door, climb up, settle in the driver's seat, and pull the door shut. He ran around to the other side sliding in beside her. Sticking the key in the ignition, Jane started up the truck giggling at the sound. Danny had purposely parked so she didn't have to back up. Both fastened their seatbelts and then Jane slowly pulled away from the curb. Even with power steering she was startled at how it felt to steer such a big vehicle. Although the truck wasn't that big, it seemed mammoth to her. Turning into a slot at the bus station, she smoothly parked, turned off the engine.

"Janie, you pass truck driving with a gold star. How did it feel?"

"I was a little apprehensive last night thinking about driving your truck, but it wasn't bad. I don't know about parking in tight spots. I'll probably park blocks away at first. But it felt good." She turned, looking out the rear window at the bed of the truck. "I'm sure there will be room for my bed, and my dresser, and the boxes."

"After the movers have loaded you up, give Dad a call to let him know you're on your way."

"Danny, your folks are beyond nice letting me store my stuff. I hope your mother doesn't mind."

"Nah. Like I said, she'll warm up to you. How could she not … you are so darn pretty," he said leaning forward, planting a peck on her plump lips. "Okay, let's find Mom and Dad, I have a bus to catch."

● ● ●

ARNIE AND MARTHA BRADLEY were sitting on a bench outside the bus terminal. They both rose when they saw their son and fiancé approaching. No one seemed to know what to say after a quick,

"Good morning. Nice day," was exchanged. Danny gripped Jane's hand as she looked around, looked at the buses lined up waiting to depart to various destinations, her eyes fixed on the one with Portsmouth above the windshield.

Martha broke the awkward silence. "Jane, what do your parents think about your engagement?"

"They didn't say a whole lot. Worried, like I guess you are I'd say. They're selling the house … moving to Los Angeles … for good."

"Oh, my. When are they scheduled to leave? I'm sure they wanted you to go with them?"

"The movers are at the house now. My parents are beginning the trip as soon as everything is loaded. They hope to get as far as Albany tonight. No … I'm not going with them."

Martha shook her head, sighed as she looked up at her husband. "What a turn of events. Not even a week since these two graduated from high school … our son leaving, Jane's parents leaving. I don't know what we're going to do without Danny's help on the farm and—"

Jane piped up surprising everyone. "I'll help. I can do it, Mrs. Bradley. I can help. With Danny's truck I can be at the farm early."

"We could use the help, Martha," Arnie said, his head cocked to the side, eyes open wide.

"All right—just a few days. Our farm hand is visiting family, asked for the week off. A week, then."

"Mom, Jane will have some boxes, a couple pieces of furniture. I asked Dad if she can store them in the cow barn. She'll have the stuff in the truck. I thought she could swing by after the movers leave. If that's all right with you, or …

"The little shed with the tractor—plenty of room there. You bring whatever you have, Jane. Arnie will help."

"I'll have a bed and a dresser, and maybe a few small pieces … boxes. You know … until I get a room, then I'll move everything there. Thank you so much, Mrs. Bradley."

The four looked up as the bus driver, a fifty something man with a shaved head wearing a gray jumpsuit, passed by calling out,

"Portsmouth. Boarding for Portsmouth." He climbed the steps taking his seat behind the wheel. Passengers queued up, mounted the steps, handed tickets to the driver.

The Bradleys hugged their son, asking him to call as soon as he knew his schedule.

Danny squeezed Jane tight to his body whispering, "I love you Janie O'Neill. See you soon as I can, hopefully before boot camp, before shipping out."

"I love you, too. I'll be waiting."

Chapter 22

————

PARKED BY THE CURB in front of her house, Jane fingered the truck's key ring, a piece of chain that less than an hour ago had been in Danny's hand. Jane watched two men carting chairs out of the kitchen, disappearing into the back of the moving van, reappearing at a gallop through the back door wedged open with a heavy block of concrete.

Putting the keys in her purse, she climbed out of the truck.

The men paid her no mind as they passed hauling her father's dresser to the van. She called to them as they reappeared.

"Hi, I'm Jane O'Neill. Did my mother, or father, tell you that my bed, mattress, and dresser go in that red truck ... over there at the curb?" she said squinting in the bright sunlight, pointing to the truck.

"No, miss. They didn't say anything."

"I'll show you my room. There are some boxes as well as the furniture. My parents will tell you it's okay. I'm staying in New Hampshire."

Jane led them through the kitchen to the hallway. Her mother was standing in the living room. "Mother, I've asked the men to put my stuff in Danny's truck."

"I see."

"Okay, Mrs. O'Neill?" one of the men asked.

"Yes, whatever she wants. She's marked her things. Jane, after you show them your room, your father and I would like a word with you."

"Sure. I'll be right back." Jane's heart raced, her body beginning to tremble. Come on, Jane. Calm down. If it doesn't work out with Danny, if he decides he doesn't want you, your father said he'll send you a train ticket. Stop this nonsense. Shake it off. You're spending the night with Cilla ... just like you've done before.

Entering her room, no longer a teenager's sanctuary, Jane pointed to the boxes. "All the furniture, mattress set, and the boxes ... all go in my truck. Do you want me to back into the driveway?"

"No, Miss O'Neill. We'll have you loaded up in no time."

Jane blew out a puff of air, relieved she didn't have to back up the truck. Why did she offer to do that? She wasn't sure she could even hit the driveway in reverse.

One man stacked three boxes in his arms, the second grabbed three more. Jane followed them down the hall as far as the living room. Her mother was sitting on a desk chair, her father leaned against the wall.

"Jane, your mother and I are sick that you have chosen to remain here. We feel you've chosen a path that will lead to heartbreak. Remember what I said the other day, if you change your mind ... whenever ... a month, a year... you are welcome to join us. We'll send you the money."

Jane's mother snatched her purse off the floor, a bare hardwood floor, as she stood up. The large Oriental rug that had delineated the rectangular living room for over fifteen years was rolled up, laid on the grass by the garage until the men packed it in the van.

"Your father and I opened a bank account for you. Here's a box of checks. You have a balance of five hundred dollars. We'll call it a graduation present."

Out of the corner of her eye she saw her dresser go by.

Jane accepted the small box her mother stretched out to her. Jane looked at the box. *This is it. Seventeen years and you're on your own. Stand tall. You can do this. Think of Danny. He's going off to fight a war. If he can do that, you can do this.* Raising her head, her eyes caught the eyes of her mother then her father. *Was that a tear she saw in her father's eye?*

Jane saw her mattress for a second as the men shuffled by the living room to the back door.

"Thank you ... for the graduation present. It's very generous. I'll try hard to spend it wisely."

"That's about it folks. Can we take that chair, Mrs. O'Neill?"

"Yes, yes, of course."

Jane backed out of the man's way.

"Well ... I hope you have a good trip." Jane pulled a piece of paper from the pocket in her capris. "Here's the Bradley's address. As you know, I'm staying with Cilla for awhile. After I get a job I'll find a place to stay. But the farm will be the best place ... if you write. Please send me your address ... when you have one."

Jane placed the small three-by-five yellow card in her mother's hand. Without thinking she wrapped her arms around her mother, then her father. They were not a demonstrative family, and were startled at the show of affection from their daughter. Shocked or not, they hugged her, then quickly dropped back.

"Bye," Jane said, looking from one to the other. "I'll write." *Strange, I said those same words earlier to Danny as he climbed on the bus. I also told him I loved him.* "I love you. Thanks for the present."

Turning away she walked out of the only home she had ever known and into the hot summer sun. Climbing into the truck, she set her purse and the box of checks on the seat beside her. Turning the key in the ignition she slowly pulled away from the curb. Checking the rearview mirror she caught her parents standing in the driveway, standing side by side. Her father's hands stuffed in his pants pocket, her mother's arms crossed over her chest. A rush of nerves raced up her arms, seized her heart. *Stop it. Stop it. Breathe slowly. You can do this.* Eyes fixed on the road her heart eased, her breathing returned to normal as Danny's image emerged, filling her mind. *I love you, Danny.*

Chapter 23

———

A WARM BREEZE RUFFLED through the sheer white curtains. Cilla, her short, flowered nightdress allowing the air to run over her bare arms and legs, leaned back against the maple headboard. She raised the icy cold bottle of pop to her lips, taking a big swallow of the fizzy drink.

Jane, dressed in the same nightdress but in a solid green, punched her pillow, plumping it up to fit the curve in her back, then settled alongside Cilla.

"Do you feel different, Cilla?"

"How do you mean?"

"High school seems years ago, but it's only been a day since we graduated."

"Older you mean?"

"Much older. You seem different. When do you leave for your vacation with your parents?"

"Next week."

Jane's heart skipped a beat. That meant she had to find a place to live in six days.

"My job starts the Monday we get back. I'm excited about it. If it holds, I'm going to be in the maternity ward with the mothers and babies."

"Are you going to stay in a dorm when you go to Michigan State?"

"I think so. Mom's checking. I haven't been assigned yet."

"Do I seem older?" Jane asked glancing at her friend. Both sipping their sodas, the girls seemed closer. The usual friction of their high school days was gone.

"Big time. How does it feel to be engaged?"

"Cilla, I love Danny so much…

"Must have been hard to say goodbye this morning. Did you do it last night?"

"Cilla, if you're asking what I think you're asking, the answer is NO." Thank heavens the room was dark. Jane could feel a flush rising over the skin of her porcelain Irish face.

"Just asking. I've done it. Night of our school dance." Cilla drank the last drop of soda putting the bottle on the nightstand. She scrunched down, elbow wedged against the pillow, resting her head on her palm facing Jane.

"Alan?"

"Yeah."

"He's nice. Do you love him?"

"I thought … maybe. But after we did it, in the backseat of his car, I knew I didn't love him."

"How was it? I mean, in the car and all."

"Not what it's cracked up to be. At first, well … he fumbled around, and I didn't know what to do. To tell you the truth, you're smart. You know you love Danny, so I'm sure it, the whole sex thing, will be way different."

Jane squirmed down under the sheet blanket. "I have to get some sleep. Tomorrow is a big day?"

"Why is that," Cilla asked, sighing as she wiggled to get comfortable.

"Besides dropping off my furniture and boxes, I'll be working on Bradley farm the next few days, helping out now that Danny is away."

"Take it easy, city girl. That could be seriously hard work. Night."

"Night, and thanks for letting me stay with you. I'll find a place in a few days."

Cilla was breathing evenly, already sound asleep.

Jane's stomach knotted, nerves pulsating through her body. Arnie's nice, but Mrs. Bradley doesn't like me. I'm sure of it. I wonder if my folks made it to Albany. What's Danny doing? He didn't call. I like the smell of the farm, the hay. Maybe Arnie will take me to the horse barn tomorrow. I miss you Danny. I love you. I'll try very hard to get your mother to like me.

Chapter 24

———

NO MATTER HOW MANY times Jane turned into Bradley Horse Farm, she marveled at the charm of the house—the dormers, the white clapboard siding, a profusion of flowers along the old fieldstone retaining wall holding back the tier of lawn, and the flower beds in front of the house. Jane desperately wanted Martha to give her the love she obviously gave her flowers.

Catching movement to her left, she saw Arnie waving her to the barn, a big grin on his face. At least Danny's father seemed to like her, accept her.

Hitting a rut, the furniture jumped in the back of the truck, scaring Jane that the bedstead might fall out. She slowed down, coasting to the spot where Arnie flagged her to park. Turning off the motor, the driver's door opened. She accepted Arnie's hand helping her down. She was dressed in her farm clothes—jeans, black T-shirt, and sneakers.

"Looks like you picked up a few things. How are you? Everything okay with your parents? Sorry. Silly question ... how could it be."

"As good as might be expected, Arnie. Where do you want me to put my stuff?" Jane pulled the bill of her new Patriot's ball cap down to shade her eyes.

"I think in the equipment shed. It's down a piece. Would you like me to drive?"

"I'm getting along pretty well. As long as I can go straight. Maybe you could give me some pointers on backing up."

"Be glad to. You climb back up behind the wheel and roll down your window. Okay, start her up. Look at both side mirrors, then the rearview. See anything?"

"No. Yes … the road behind me," she said laughing.

"Right. Put her in reverse and give her a little gas, get the feel, then let up on the gas."

Jane did as she was told, feeling the truck respond. Stopping, she smiled at Arnie.

"Okay. See that grassy patch to the left? Turn the wheel and back onto the grass and stop." Arnie walked alongside the truck watching her.

Jane was relaxed as she looked into the side mirror letting up on the gas.

Walking quickly to the passenger door, Arnie hopped in. "Nicely done, Miss O'Neill. Did you get the feel of the size of the truck? The weight? What it took to move her?"

"Yes, I did," she said grinning. "Now, where is that shed you were talking about?"

"Just drive by the barn. When you backed up, the fork to the right of the barn is straight ahead. One thing to watch for when you're navigating around the farm is a hole. I knew you were okay on that particular piece of grass, but you always want to check, walk around, until you get a feel for not only the truck but the land. Now, little lassie, let's head down to the shed and get your stuff unloaded."

Jane slowly followed the road, a well-worn path, to the shed. Coming into view, it was not what she'd call a shed, rather a good-sized garage.

"Let's see you back up in front of that sliding door on the right," Arnie said. Jumping to the ground, he strolled to the shed's door sliding it open.

Jane turned off the engine and climbed down. Walking around the truck, taking note of how she was going to turn around to be in position to back up to the opening. Satisfied she had a plan, she returned to her seat behind the wheel, started the engine and navigated to a perfect position with the back end a couple yards in front of the open door.

Grinning, flashing thumbs up to Jane, the pair began transferring her things from the truck to the shed. "You may be thin but you have muscles, girl. Are you sure you can hold up the other end of that dresser? We can wait for Martha—"

"I can do it. But maybe pull out a couple of the drawers."

Martha sauntered up, looked from Jane hauling her headboard into the shed, to her husband.

"Hi, Mrs. Bradley."

"Enough room, Arnie?" Martha asked, a scowl across her face.

A chill ran up Jane's arm but just as quickly a whoosh of warm air enveloped her blunting Martha's chilly non-greeting. Setting the headboard next to the dresser, she turned to Martha. "What time do you want me to start tomorrow morning?"

"You don't have to come over … take a few days off."

"But, from what Danny told me, on a farm there are always chores to be done … 24 / 7 he said." Jane tried to lighten the air, tried to laugh but it caught in her throat sounding more like a gurgle.

"Sure enough, Jane," Arnie said. "How about we start her in the hen house, Martha? Get to know Daisy?"

"Daisy?"

"Our big mother hen. She's a layer that one. More eggs out of her than any of the others. Come on over nine-ish, have a cup of coffee, then Martha will introduce you to Daisy. Okay, Martha?"

"I suppose so. No hurry, Jane."

Chapter 25

———

CILLA'S BREATHING WAS SOFT and rhythmic.

Creeping out of bed, Jane picked up her clothes and tote off the chair where she had laid them the night before. Clutching the tote that held the check from her parents, Jane tiptoed to the bathroom changing into her jeans and blue T-shirt and left the house. The noise of the truck's engine kicking in was going to wake the household up but it couldn't be helped.

It was six o'clock. Arnie said to come over at nine, said there was no need to rush. But Jane wanted to make a good impression and she was certain the Bradleys would be up. She wasn't the only one missing Danny. It was going to be a hard day for his parents as well—their only son leaving for the Army the day before yesterday.

Turning up the driveway there was Arnie standing on the grass by the back door waving to her, a wide grin on his face. Jane had guessed right to come early. She was now the official stand in for Danny.

"Good morning, Arnie. Nice day to meet Daisy don't you think?"

Jane's eyes sparkled, a slight moistness building under her lids as Arnie gave her a hug.

"Daisy will love to meet you. Martha and I were about to sit down for our first cup of coffee. Come join us."

Suzy and Dog scampered up to the humans, Dog always in the lead, Suzy always following on paws turned out, ears flopping, eager for biscuits. Jane petted, cooed to them in turn. Fishing around the bottom of her tote, she came up with a doggie treat for each, their tails raking the grass, waiting for more. Showing an empty palm, Dog took off down the path, Suzy in his wake, both disappearing behind bales of hay.

Chuckling at the dogs, Arnie rested his arm around Jane's shoulders as they entered the house. "Martha, look who I found out the back door. She thinks it's time to meet Daisy. Pour the girl a cup of coffee and then you two can go to the hen house."

"Good morning, Mrs. Bradley."

"Hello, Jane. No need to come so early. Now that you're here ... no need to be formal ... call me Martha."

"Thank you ... Martha. I was awake and I had an inkling you would both be up."

"That's such a pretty ring that son of mine gave you," Arnie said, holding Jane's hand up, her fingers curling around his palm. "Martha, you still have that gold chain of your mother's?"

"Yes. It's in the drawer of my jewelry case I believe. Haven't opened that drawer in a long time."

"How about you loan it to Jane. She's not going to part with that ring but maybe around her neck—"

"Oh, no. Please, don't—"

"Nonsense," Arnie replied. "Out on the farm you don't know what you're going to step in, get on your fingers. Martha?"

"I'm going. I'm going."

Arnie winked at Jane over the rim of his coffee mug.

"Here. This what you're looking for?" Martha laid the gold chain on the table.

"That's it. What do you say, Jane? When you're busy with Daisy, and ... the horse barn for instance, I'm sure Danny wouldn't mind if you wore the ring on this chain."

Jane looked at Martha who instantly looked away. "You're very kind. And, you're right. I'd die if the stone got one spec of ...

of dirt on it." Sucking in a breath, holding it, she slipped the ring off, laying it in Arnie's outstretched palm.

"Martha, how about you put the ring on the chain, and I'll fasten it on our son's fiancée."

● ● ●

BEFORE LEAVING THE HOUSE, Martha tore off a sheet of paper toweling placing it in the bottom of a metal wire egg basket with a wood handle. A basket large enough for a dozen eggs she explained. In the dim gray light of dawn, Jane followed Martha down the path.

Martha unlatched the door of the chicken's empty pen, a large space secured with a wire fence—all around and over the top to keep predators out of the yard.

"Here, put on these gloves. A hen can be ornery, peck at your hand when you reach for her eggs."

Martha latched the wire gate then opened the door to the coop. Cackling hens and a rooster rushed out doing the quick step on webbed feet, raising a ruckus for food.

Martha's lips formed a hint of a smile which she quickly stifled. "Before gathering the eggs, we'll scoop out cracked corn for their food bins—three of them—you can spot them around the pen. They're made of heavy rubber so they won't flip over. You do that while I refresh their water, then we'll gather the eggs."

"The chickens are very pretty, Martha. So many colors— yellow, gray, beautiful red and touches of black. I've only seen pictures of yellow baby chicks."

"Over thirty of them, different types and breeds."

"I thought they'd look the same. And the rooster certainly struts like he owns the place. Which one is Daisy?"

"She's in the coop, still nesting. That's why the gloves. She's liable to give you a peck and I don't mean on the cheek," Martha said with a little chuckle.

Jane didn't look up at the slight crack in Martha's chilly manner. *Maybe she's warming up to me,* she thought. *Oh, I hope so.*

"The chickens don't seem to be afraid of you, Jane. The real test is Daisy. Let's go in the coop. The nests are built up off the ground so they have some peace from the rest of the brood. There she is, in her little spot. Go ahead, slowly push your hand under her. She usually lays two or three eggs. Go on. Your glove is protecting your hand in case she—"

Daisy's head jerked around but she didn't peck at the glove. Jane carefully pulled her hand out with an egg, whispering softly to Daisy that she wasn't going to hurt her.

Martha stood to the side her eyes following her apprentice. "Nicely done, Jane. I think you have a new friend. We're finished here. Let's take the eggs up to the house."

Martha latched the swinging door to the chicken's yard, the hens cackling, racing around, strutting, stopping, pecking at a food bin. Leaving the cackling chickens, the two women sauntered along the path to the house, Jane carrying the egg basket.

"Your house is beautiful, Martha. It's so big sitting up on the rise." Jane stopped, held up her hand to shield her eyes from the morning sun, looking out over the farm.

"It is big. Arnie and I wanted a large family but it was not to be. We were blessed with one son, a little Arnold. Thank God for him, but there were no more. After Danny there were problems, female problems. I couldn't have any more children." Martha paused looking wistfully at her home on the hill. "The house was built in 1840 by Danny's great, great grandfather. Arnie and I hoped to fill it with the laughter of little brothers and sisters."

Martha sighed, continued up the path, Suzy and Dog sprinting ahead.

Jane caught up. "What time do you usually tend to the chickens? I can help."

"Twice a day—early morning and mid-afternoon. Sunday ... not so early."

"What is early? Four-thirty? Five?"

"Five is good."

Chapter 26

———

SUNBEAMS PEEKED THROUGH the leaves of a stand of birch trees, turning the bark to silver. Swinging into the driveway, Jane sighed taking in the beauty of the farm. It reminded her of a Currier and Ives painting. She could envision the big farmhouse after a heavy snowfall—a wedding cake with peaks of whipped egg whites atop the dormers, red barns and sheds dotting the landscape.

She glanced at her watch—5:05 a.m.

Reversing direction, she headed straight for the chicken coop, the truck bumping over the ruts. Climbing out of the truck, smiling at the quiet pen, she unlatched the gate, latching it again behind her. Opening the coop door, she was greeted with a marching flurry of feathers—yellow, black, red, gray. The chickens strutted out into the fenced pen cawing in deep raspy chicken speak. Freedom at last.

Arnie hopped in his Ford station wagon, black with wood-like side panels, and headed down to the coop, following BigRed. He came up with the nickname for Danny's truck after showing the diminutive lass how to back up. He chuckled at the plucky girl, clucking back at her new feathered friends. Climbing out of the car, he called out a greeting, a mug of coffee in each hand. "Good morning, Jane. Martha saw you driving over to the hen house and perked a pot of coffee real quick," he said handing her a mug as she poured a scoop of corn into the last of the rubber feeders.

"Thanks, smells wonderful. Umm, tastes even better."

"Hop in my car. I told Martha I was going to show you the horse barn, add to your chores," he said with a wink. "Draw down a few sips of that coffee. Can't say as I won't be hitting any bumps along the way."

Entering the barn, the scent of fresh hay tickled her nose. Two large horse heads poked out over the half doors of the stalls. Their big, soft dark eyes followed the humans. Arnie handed two apples to Jane. "Their morning treat. Offer it to Mildred. You met her on your first visit to the farm."

Mildred nodded her head up and down, then carefully nuzzled the apple from Jane's palm. Without thinking, Jane reached up, her fingers running down the mare's furry white star to her soft nose. "Good morning, Mildred. Remember me? I'm Jane. If we play our cards right, I'll be down to see you every day."

"You also met Sir Charles the day Danny brought you to the farm, but now you'll get to know him—his beauty, the majesty of a fine racehorse. When he and I are alone I call him Charlie but he doesn't like me to address him as Charlie when anyone else is around."

"Oh, I see. So, Sir Charles, we have to become fast friends then maybe you'll let me call you *Charlie* without causing a fuss," she whispered.

"To start you with the art of grooming a fine horse, we'll bring Mildred out of her stall. You're new to horses so be careful. I don't want your foot smashed under a hoof. Open Mildred's door, grasp her bridle, give a slight tug. She'll follow. We'll clip a rope to each side of her halter holding her in place in the center aisle of the barn." Arnie clipped one side, nodded to Jane to clip the other.

"Good, now follow me to the tack room. You'll find there are several types of brushes. Your job will be to use a body brush, brushing Mildred down every day. She likes this and will be happy whenever she sees you come in the barn. This is the body brush— oval, soft bristles made of horse hair, a strap around the top to slide your hand under as you grip it. Come on back to Mildred and I'll show you. Mildred's gentle. She'll be under your care until you get familiar with the horses.

"Start with the top of her neck and work your way to her rear. Switch sides and repeat. Always be sure she's wearing her halter before bringing her out of the stall."

Arnie stroked Mildred's neck. "Leave the mane. We'll get a special comb when you finish with her coat. Okay, you try it and then I'm going to groom Sir Charles in his stall." Arnie stepped aside, handing the brush to Jane. Without hesitation she mimicked his stroke—length of the stroke and the pressure.

Arnie stepped into Charlie's stall, grooming him with longer strokes and applying more pressure. Charlie raised his nose up and down delighting in the brushing.

"Arnie, what about your dad, Danny's grandfather? I can see there is so much to be done on a farm. Did you like helping him?" Jane called out.

"Oh, my dad, he was something else. He lived life on the edge. Gambled, raced horses and cars. Did you notice the painting in the living room, over the fireplace?" Arnie stood a moment in the stall's doorway watching Jane. "My great grandfather won it in a poker game. It's an original Picasso. At least that's what he claimed. Galleries advertise it as modern art—the bodies, faces are distorted.

"It seems the value of his work goes up every year. He was just emerging as an artist forty years ago when Dad won the thing. Now it's worth several hundred dollars. Martha looked up his work recently … some of his paintings go for over a thousand. He's still alive. I like the simplicity of his paintings, the vibrant colors, but Martha is not a fan. Keeps saying she's going to sell it, or wrap it up and put it in the back barn along with all the old furniture collected over the years. Collected since my dad's great grandfather, Danny's great, great, grandfather, Marshall Bradley, bought the land. He was a young guy barely thirty when he built the house. Died at age seventy, at least that's what I was told."

Chapter 27

———

THE INTERCOM MOUNTED on the post outside Charlie's stall crackled to life.

"Arnie, lunch is ready." Martha's garbled voice perked up the stallion's ears.

With four long strides, Arnie pushed the button under the mesh speaker. "We'll be right up."

Sir Charles pawed at the straw signaling he wanted more brushing. Arnie latched the stall door. "It's okay, big guy. I'll be back. Come on, lass. When Martha says it's lunchtime we make fast tracks to the house. How long since you ate something? And that mug of coffee I gave you earlier doesn't count. Do you mind if I call you lass? You're such a pretty Irish girl it just seems right. I tell you, that son of mine showed some smarts asking you to marry him."

"I like it … you're calling me a lass." Jane smiled at Arnie. Danny looked so much like his dad and he certainly inherited his friendly, charming manner. Checking her watch, her brows shot up. She flashed a grin at Arnie. "I can't believe it—noon already. I devoured a candy bar I found in the glove compartment on my way to the farm. Danny must have left it. I guess that makes it seven hours. I'm right behind you."

• • •

THE KITCHEN WAS FILLED with the scent of garlic, onion, and tomato. Jane had never smelled anything so good. Feeding the chickens and pulling the brush along Mildred's hide, made her sweat in the summer heat. She was starving. Her usual orange would never have satisfied her hunger pangs.

She watched Martha place a slice of thick hearty bread in the bottom of each bowl, ladling the soup over the bread just shy of the rim. As she ladled the soup, Jane took each bowl to the table.

Standing at the table, she hesitated. Where should she sit?

Arnie nodded at a chair. "Sit there, Jane. Danny generally sits on the other side. I say he sits, but he's usually on the run somewhere and stands at the counter to eat."

"Now, Arnold, don't go telling tales. It's perfectly all right if the boy wants to stand."

Arnie's eyes widened at the rebuke. His wife had always nagged at their son to sit. Meals were to be enjoyed as a family, with conversation.

Jane realized that the few minutes of shared words at the hen house had not softened Martha's attitude toward her one bit.

Arnie didn't waste any time diving his soup spoon into the thickening soup, swirling the bread, breaking it up, then into his mouth. Jane mimicked his actions. "Umm, Martha, this is wonderful. The bread—"

She was interrupted by the ring of the wall phone next to the refrigerator. Arnie pushed his chair back, picked up the black receiver. "Son, what a wonderful surprise—"

"Dad, I'm coming home. I was assigned to an equipment maintenance detail, Fort Benning, Georgia. But the slot won't be open for a week. The Sergeant signing me in said that with my experience with farm machinery he knew a perfect assignment, a place where I'd be welcome, fit in. He made a couple of telephone calls to make it happen. He told me to go home for five days. He gave me some forms with the information of where and when I was to report at Fort Benning."

"Son, that's wonderful. We'll save you a bowl of your mom's tomato soup," his dad said chuckling, exchanging a smile with Martha.

"Dad, is Jane there?"

"Sure is. A real worker she is. Here, I'll put her on."

Jane wasn't sure if Arnie meant she should take the receiver or Martha. She looked anxiously at Arnie until he waved the receiver at her. Jumping from her chair, she grasped the phone, holding it to her ear.

"Janie, are you there?"

"Yes, are you okay?"

"Yeah, I'm okay. I'm at the Portsmouth bus station. Dad will fill you in, but I have five days before I have to report. I'll be home in a couple of hours. Can you meet me?"

"Of course, we'll meet you. What time?"

"3:10."

"You sound like something's wrong?"

"No, no. Everything is fine. Janie?"

"Yes ... I'm here."

"I want to get married."

"I know, we—"

"No, no. Not Christmas. Tomorrow or the day after. As soon as we can arrange it unless you want a big wedding—church, a white dress?"

Jane didn't know what to say. Her brows furrowed, eyes darting from Danny's mom to his dad.

"Janie?"

She had to make a decision. Her heart was racing. She looked out the window at the landscape, the farm lying out in the sunshine. "No, Danny. Wait, no to a big wedding. Yes to getting married. Danny. I'll tell your mom and dad. Okay?"

"More than okay. I love you Janie."

"I love you, Danny."

Jane returned the receiver to the hook, took a deep breath, and with wide eyes, lips parting in a big smile, she relayed their son's words. "Danny wants us to be married as soon as possible, within the next three days."

Martha sat stunned. Her husband sprang from his seat, enveloping his future daughter-in-law in a bear hug, rocking her back and forth.

Chapter 28

———

ADRENALIN SHOT THROUGH Jane's body.

Married!

Danny asked me to marry him. Now!

Dog, snoozing under the table, lifted his head, groaned, stretched, laying back on the floor.

A flush to her face, a feeling of warmth up her arm, Jane caressed the diamond on her ring finger. She wanted to dance, shout to the world—*Danny and I are getting married.*

It took all her willpower to remain seated.

Arnie paced over the black and white linoleum squares of the large farmhouse kitchen. One glance at Martha sitting stiff, eyes boring holes in the cabinet behind Jane, told him his wife was not on board with this wedding. He grabbed the phonebook off the top of the refrigerator, thumbed through the pages, then dialed the telephone. "Town Clerk, please," he said glancing again at Martha, then Jane, then out the window. "Yes, hello. What time do you close this afternoon? ...5:00? If my son and his fiancée were there by four could they get a marriage license today?" Arnie continued to look out the window listening to the person on the other end. "And what is the fee?"

Arnie returned the phone to the cradle, again he snatched the phonebook, thumbing through the pages. Laying the book on the kitchen table, he pulled the curly telephone cord to its maximum length. Jane reached across the table to hold the book open to the page Arnie was looking at. He looked up, smiled, then back to the page as he dialed.

"Hank, Arnold Bradley here. How are you? …Happy to hear it. Say, Hank, my son is leaving for Fort Benning in a few days. Yes, the Army. Hank, I know you're retired, but you were the first minister I thought of. Remember, you married Martha and me? That's right. Well my son is engaged to a most charming girl, make that a most charming woman. They want to get married in the next three days … before he has to report for duty. Can you perform the ceremony—probably this Saturday, maybe Sunday?"

Arnie let out a hearty laugh. "Yes, I know this younger generation … always in a hurry. My son will call you this evening, if that's okay."

Hanging up the phone, he turned to his wife. "How about that, Martha? If Danny agrees, he and Jane can be married by the same minister who presided over our wedding. Isn't that wonderful?"

"Yes. Wonderful." Her words were spoken in a whisper.

Jane couldn't tell if she was mad, sad, or just resigned. As for herself, she couldn't stop grinning.

Martha picked up her empty soup bowl and coffee cup, putting them on the counter next to the sink.

"Martha, can I use the bathroom. I have a clean shirt in the truck. I'd like to freshen up before meeting Danny, unless you have something you'd like me to do."

"No. You go ahead. Arnie, we should leave for the bus station in an hour. From what I heard on this end of your conversation with the Town Clerk, we'd better take Jane and Danny to get the license." Martha turned to Jane who was still grinning as she cleared the dishes. The girl looked as if she would float through the air any minute, defying gravity as well as the enormity of the step she was to take. "Jane, are you sure this is what you want? What about your parents? Unless they call you don't even have a way of reaching them. Or, do you?"

"I can leave a message at the new offices of my father's company. They'll still be on their way to Los Angeles, but at least they'll know … once my father goes to his office. Martha, in answer to your question, is this what I want? Yes, it is. Danny and I had planned to be married so if it's not Christmas, I'm happy, more than happy, to marry your son now."

"Jane, a new plan," Arnie said. "You take the truck. We'll follow in the car. After we hug our boy, you and Danny can go on to get the license while Martha and I return to the farm. I'm sure you two will have some things to talk about."

Arnie unable to contain himself again wrapped a giggling bride-to-be in a bear hug.

Chapter 29

———

THE BUS PULLED INTO the station, hissed, blew out air, and came to a standstill. Danny was the first passenger to hop off. He made a beeline to the perky redhead waving both arms in the air. Lifting her, twirling her in the air, he finally set her on the ground, giving her a passionate smooch. "I love you, Janie." Giving her another quick kiss on her smiling lips, he grasped her hand in a tight grip.

"Danny, I look awful. I was working at the farm feeding Daisy, brushing Mildred and, well … I didn't have time to run to Cilla's to change my clothes, so—"

Danny pressed his lips to hers. "Janie, you always look beautiful."

She giggled, "Well, thankfully, I did have a clean shirt in the truck."

His mom and dad were next—a hug for his dad, a kiss and a hug for his mom before grasping Jane's hand again. "Mom, Dad, let's grab a cup of coffee at the café across the street," Danny said lifting Jane's hand to his lips. Not waiting for his parent's answer, he and Jane led the way.

The café was *their* café, where they began falling in love, and now they were planning their wedding.

"Danny, Jane, hi. Booth three?"

"You got that right, Kathy, and four cups of *strong* coffee," Danny said letting Jane scoot first into the booth. "We have some serious plans to make."

Kathy hastened her steps, returning with the coffees, creamers and sugar packets. "Sandwiches?"

"Not today, Kathy. We won't be here long. Maybe tomorrow. Dad, you said the Town Clerk will be there until five?"

"That's right, son. You have to have a form of ID—driver's license, or birth certificate. They will ask for your Social Security number. The marriage license will set you back forty-five bucks but there's no waiting period."

"Okay, it's Thursday. Thanks, Kathy." Danny slid the mugs across the table to his mom and dad, and one to Jane. "Janie, can we be ready by … by Saturday, Sunday at the latest? I have to leave Monday on the 4:30 bus. Can we do it?"

"Danny, we can do anything. I'll start a list. Besides what I'm going to wear, I have to ask Cilla to be my bridesmaid, and I have to find a room to rent. Cilla is leaving with her parents Monday afternoon."

"Do you remember that dance the school held last year—that barn outside of Manchester? Smithfield Farm I believe. My band was hired to play. Oh, gosh, that reminds me. I have to call Tommy. Get the boys together. We have to have dancing at our wedding. He'll spread the word to the guys and—"

"And Cilla will tell the girls. How many? We have to be careful of the cost. Cilla and I can make sandwiches—little finger ones. I saw them in a magazine—"

"And I'll buy a couple kegs of beer. Tommy will haul the kegs to Smithfield … I'm sure. Excuse me a minute while I call Tommy with the big news and get him going on preparations to be my best man. Tommy's in for a workout." Danny looked around for the payphone, spotted it, and hustled over to make his call.

Five minutes later, a beaming groom-to-be returned to the booth, sat back looking at the notes he had made on the back of the café's placemat. He glanced up at his parents and then Janie. "Tommy's good to go."

"You make my head spin, you two," Arnie said chuckling.

Martha remained silent. Her eyes shifting from her son to the girl he was going to marry in three days. Her hands were in her lap, spine straight, coffee untouched.

"What do you think, Mom? Are you okay?"

"Seems I have to be … okay. You've made your plans. But I don't see why you can't wait until you get out of the service? This is all so … so sudden. You barely know each other."

"Now, now, Martha, it seems to me I remember a certain young girl, nineteen you were, I believe. I didn't want anyone else snatching you away from me."

"Humph. I was almost twenty."

"There. You see. We were practically the same age as Danny and Jane. Of course, I was the older man—twenty-one if memory serves me right."

"Your parents were furious with us."

"Worked out didn't it," Arnie reached for his wife's hand. "Well, didn't it?"

"Yes, but that was then and this is now. Somehow Danny and Jane seem a lot younger than we were."

"Well, Janie and I have to run. We have a marriage license to get. Maybe we can walk down memory lane with you another time."

"I'll get the coffees," Arnie said. "You run along. When your mom and I get home, I'll check on the Smithfield Barn. Could be booked this time of year."

"Oh, and Dad, they have cottages. See if they have one we could stay in after the wedding, one night? And confirm the minister. I always liked Hank but never dreamed he'd be performing my wedding."

Arnie laughed. "Anything else, son?"

"Not at the moment. Come on, Janie. Let's go get our license. Thanks, Mom and Dad," he called over his shoulder as he held the café door for Jane, and then held the truck door sneaking a quick peck on her cheek as he gave her a hand up into BigRed.

Chapter 30

———

"CILLA. YOU AWAKE?"

Cilla bolted upright off her pillow. "Of course, I'm awake. Where have you been? I didn't dare call Bradley farm. I was afraid I'd get Danny's mother. I almost called the hospital. I thought maybe you were in an accident. It's not like you not to call."

Jane scooched onto the bed next to her friend hips bumping.

"Will you be my bridesmaid?"

Cilla drew her knees up. "I already said I would. Of course, it depends."

"Depends? On what?"

"I may not be home for Christmas ... Michigan State is pretty far away. I still can't believe I was accepted. When my folks go on vacation, we're going to look at the dorms, other stuff. If I don't like it, my mom said I can withdraw my application. But ... I'll probably be home for the holidays."

"Saturday or Sunday. *This* Saturday or Sunday!"

Jane squirmed around, drew up her knees to face Cilla.

"Danny came home today. It was unexpected to say the least. Oh, Cilla, he is so handsome ... I love him so much. Seems he has five days before he has to report to Fort Benning. That's the Army base where's he's going for boot camp. The Army is assigning him to the armored tank division, machine maintenance because of his work on the farm equipment. I figure ... well, that sounds safe don't you think. Working on equipment?"

"I guess so. But, oh my God, Jane are you sure? I mean so fast. How can you possibly plan a—"

"It's done. Mr. Bradley called a minister friend—he's retired. Danny and I drove to the Town Clerk's office. Cilla we got the marriage license—right then."

"Wow. What about Mrs. Bradley? Hey, you're going to be a Mrs. Bradley. What did Danny's mom say?"

"Nothing. She said nothing except *why the rush*. Then Mr. B. spoke right up. Cilla, Mrs. B. was nineteen and he was twenty-one when they got married. She's in shock. Her face never changed. And, you know that barn, the one where the Junior Prom was held? In Manchester."

"I'll never forget it. Billy Hutchinson kissed me that night," Cilla said giggling. "Awkward. Very awkward. He had no idea how to kiss."

"Oh, yeah. Like you're an expert."

"I certainly knew I didn't like it. That barn was cute. But it might be booked ... summer parties and all."

"Arnie already called. They aren't booked on Sunday ... they were but they had a cancellation ... and ... they have little cottages. They told Arnie the cottages were taken, but when Mr. B. said that he'd have to find another place for his son's wedding ... well, they told him they were painting one by the lake. The man said they'd stop the painting ... outside he said ... and could have the inside clean and ready for us. And—"

"Wait. Jane, do you really want to do this ... marry a farmer. I mean the whole farm thing? You said you liked going out to the farm but this is for real. You'll be a farmer's wife—pigs, chickens ... tractors. Hard work."

Jane smiled thinking of Daisy. She'd laid three beautiful eggs this morning. Daisy lifted her fat feathered tummy on her spindly legs so Jane could carefully reach in to retrieve the prizes. "They don't have pigs. At least I haven't seen any."

"Stop joking. Where are you going to live? Have you found a place?"

"I haven't had a chance, but I saw a sign in the window next to the pharmacy—Room for Rent."

"I'm leaving with my parents on Monday. Mom asked me today to be sure to remind you to move out by Sunday."

Jane flung her legs off the bed. "I know. Let me remind you ... you're booked to be my bridesmaid on Sunday. You can bring a date, if you like. Night, night, bridesmaid."

Jane pulled the sheet up as both girls turned off the bedside lamps.

"Wow, Jane. You're getting married," Cilla whispered, the room washed in moonlight. "I guess you'll be doing it."

Jane punched Cilla's arm. "Is that all you ever think about?"

"Just sayin, Jane. Just sayin."

Chapter 31

———

AS EARLY THE NEXT MORNING as he dared, Danny picked Jane up at Cilla's. Putting the truck in high gear, the couple raced back to the farm. Laughing, his arm around his fiancée and with a quick peck on her cheek, they entered the farmhouse.

One look at Martha, Jane wiped the grin off her face.

Arnie jumped out of his chair and put his empty coffee mug in the sink. "Come on, son. Let's go check on Sir Charles."

"Dad, how about we stay—"

"Hey, come on. Humor your dad. Sir Charles misses you. Your mom and Jane will be just fine." Arnie hugged Jane, and with a kiss on Martha's cheek, exited stage left. Jane smiled recognizing his attempt to flee. She had been in a play in the sixth grade, and the teacher always said to *exit stage left* when you want to escape a situation.

Jane ambled to the coffee pot, a smile back on her face. "Can I top off your cup, Martha?"

"Yes, that would be nice. I have a couple of things to go over with you ... now that it seems you'll be joining the family." Her hands wrapped around the hot mug as Jane took a seat across from her. "I'm putting my reservations aside, Jane. After all, it's Danny's decision to marry ... to marry, so ..." She sighed. "His father and I had a long talk last night after Danny went to bed. If what I'm about to say doesn't feel appropriate, we'll drop the subject."

Another sigh escaped her open mouth, deeper this time. A veil of apprehension creeping into the lines on her face, Martha looked into Jane's eyes. The girl was sitting at attention. "It isn't proper for a young bride to live alone in the city."

Jane shook her head. "Martha, I'll—"

"This house is very large. Arnold and I had hoped to fill it with children, but that was not to be except for our precious son. We have plenty of room, and we both thought you might like to move into the guest bedroom. Of course, there are five bedrooms, plus Arnie's and mine, so it doesn't have to be the one we call the guest bedroom. You can select any of the five."

Jane's hand shot across the table laying her palm on top of Martha's clasped hands. "Martha, are you sure? I love the farm. I haven't told you yet—I'm going to take some business courses, at the University of New Hampshire in Durham. And, I'm going to apply for a job at the university ... maybe in the cafeteria. If you really want me to stay, I promise I won't be a bother ... that is unless you change your mind or, if I move in and it doesn't work out, then you must tell me."

"Jane, I'm sure you will not be a bother. There is one more thing, and this time you are the one to say if you don't like it."

"What ... I can't imagine—"

"Arnie reminded me of my wedding dress. It's stored in a cedar chest in the attic. When he and I were married I was about your size. Of course, I've filled out a little since then, here and there," she said with a hint of a smile. "Come on, Jane. Let's take a look. You must understand it's been years so the dress is a bit old fashioned—white lace, high neck, no plunging neckline."

Jane shook her head, "Absolutely not. I wouldn't wear a plunging neckline at my wedding."

The farmhouse was built with two staircases to the second floor, then another flight of stairs to two more rooms with dormers, and one more staircase to the attic.

Martha led the way up the steep creaky stairs to the attic, both she and Jane grasping the handrail—Martha to keep her balance and Jane to keep from tripping when her head emerged from the staircase. Her eyes darted around the enormous space piled high with furniture, crates, and boxes. Light filtered in either end through two lace-covered windows.

"Martha, where did all this …. this furniture … and stuff … come from?"

"You must remember, Jane, this house was built by a Bradley a long time ago, eighteen hundreds—Danny's great, great grandfather. Over the years, babies were born, grew up, and ventured out on their own. Each generation worked hard as children on the farm, but then went off to seek their fortune. Danny is the only one who has shown an interest in the farm, at least that's what I've been told. Danny built a few pieces of furniture in a shop class, but then gave it up. He was good at it, good at bringing out the grain, the beauty of the wood. Watch your head, Jane. There's a lot of room up here but not much headroom. Here's the cedar chest. Help me slide it out would you, so we can open it?"

Martha pulled a towel from her apron, wiped the dust off the top of the chest tucking the cloth back under her apron's tie.

"Help me lift the lid, Jane. It won't fall back. There are leather straps securing the lid to the box. This was my hope chest, where I started to collect items my mother thought a bride should have. You won't have time for such a tradition. Here, pick up the end of this dress bag. We'll hang it on one of the rafters."

"Can I unzip it, Martha?"

"Go ahead. Remember, you don't have to be polite. Just tell me if it isn't to your liking."

Jane pulled the zipper down, folded the bag back, her fingers reaching to touch the soft ecru lace. "It's so delicate, so soft."

"It's made of silk. My mother sewed every stitch for me."

"The seed pearls … Martha, this gown is beautiful, too beautiful. I couldn't even think of wearing such a treasure."

"Nonsense. Let's see if it fits. Slip off your T-shirt and shorts. I'll lift it over your head."

Jane felt a whisper of air as the gown floated over her blossoming frame.

Martha caught her breath, her hand slowly covering her mouth.

Jane felt a tear gather in her eye. She quickly brushed it away. "Oh, Martha, I would be honored to wear this dress. I think it fits perfectly, don't you? Even the length is perfect," she said preening to see her reflection—front, side, and back—in the large dusty oval mirror in a gilded frame.

"Yes, dear. It fits *perfectly*."

Chapter 32

———

"HEY, YOU TWO, come on down. We could do with your input."

"I guess we're needed. Amazing how the sound travels up the staircases," Jane said running her fingers over the milky seed pearls.

"Arnie's voice can be booming. Here, let me help you out of the dress. We'll put it back in the bag. I'm afraid you'll have to take it to the cleaners so they can get the cedar smell out. Warn them about the silk—all these years. It's very delicate."

"Oh, I will. I'll have them promise on their life that they won't harm it."

"Well, I don't think on their life," Martha said zipping up the garment bag. "I'll let you carry it down. But watch the steps. Some can be tricky."

Jane and Martha walked into the kitchen to find the boy and the man hunched over the kitchen table, each with a pad of paper. Arnie looked up. "Whatcha got there, lass?"

"Only the most beautiful wedding gown in the whole wide world. A gown I might add that you, Daniel Bradley, cannot see, not even a peek, until we are standing in front of the minister."

Arnie winked at his wife. "That reminds me, son. What are you going to wear on the most important day of your life?"

"I don't know. Mom, what about that blazer you bought me … for the Junior Prom?"

"No, I think you should wear a suit. Arnie, what about that black suit of yours? You and Danny go see if it fits. If it does bring it out so it can go to the cleaners to be pressed along with Jane's dress."

Watching her son walk away with his father, Martha's heart skipped a beat. *Army, married, so grown up.*

Martha slid onto the chair vacated by her husband pulling his notepad in front of her. Her brows furrowed reading the list of things that had to be done before Sunday—only two days away. "We don't know how many will show up for the wedding, but with Tommy asking Danny's best friends—"

"That would be the whole school—captain of the football team bringing home two championships in a row, and then basketball." Jane grinned, sitting in front of Danny's scribbled notepad, tapping his pen on the top sheet, trying to decipher his writing.

"What about your friend, Cilla isn't it? Did you ask her to call around?"

"I only have a few friends … nothing like Danny. I was considered a nerd. No one wanted to have anything to do with me."

"Nonsense, a pretty girl like you?" Martha shook her head, missing the astonished look on Jane's face. Other than saying the dress fit perfectly she really hadn't said anything complimentary since the day Danny introduced them.

"Martha, I'm going to make a call if you don't mind. Check if my parents have arrived, if my father's in the office."

"Go ahead. I'll be adding to Arnie's list."

Jane retrieved the slip of paper from her wallet with her father's new telephone number and dialed.

"Hello, is Mr. O'Neill there? This is his daughter Jane. …Oh, he's not expected until Monday. Do you have a number … a motel, someplace where I might reach him? …I see. Well, I guess the only thing I can do is leave a message. Tell him I'm sorry I have to let him know this way, but my fiancé, Danny, has to report to Fort Benning, and well … we're getting married this Sunday … well

… the Bradleys have offered me their guest bedroom … so … my father has their telephone number. You'll be sure to give him my message? … Thank you."

Martha stood, walked to the sink, and looked out the window. She closed her eyes listening to Jane's end of the conversation. *The poor girl, but at least she tried.*

"Well, Martha, I'll tell Danny I tried." Jane sat back staring at the notepad.

Martha looked down at the sink, turned on the faucet, turned off the faucet. Returning to the table, she picked up Arnie's pen. "Food. A buffet, because we have no idea how many will show up but we do know they are all going to be young people, and young people like to eat. By the way, I checked the weather report this morning and Sunday should be nice. You can say your vows by the lake. That will be lovely. Everyone can stand. No need to cart around chairs. Then in Smithfield's barn—"

"There are plenty of folding chairs and several long tables for the buffet. I know because I helped on the prom committee. They have a storage room at the end of the barn—"

"Good. I was going to ask Arnie to pick up some watermelons—nice on a hot summer day, but watermelon can be messy. I'll call the grocer, ask him to make up a bowl of melon balls for … how many … thirty, maybe forty?"

"That should be more than enough … I guess," Jane said. "I've never planned anything like this … a big party. I've never even been to a wedding."

"Chips, dips, finger sandwiches, and, oh yes, I'll ask the grocer to bake up two sheet cakes. If there are only twenty, each guest can have a big piece of cake. If more than twenty, they get little pieces. What do you think, Jane?"

"Cilla will come over to help make the sandwiches. I'm sure she will. But, Martha, I think this is getting to be expensive and my parents are somewhere between here and California. But maybe they would send some money afterward … after they get over the shock. Martha, I have money they gave me for graduation. With your kind offer of a room, I'll give you all of it. Five hundred dollars."

Martha looked up, her eyes blinking rapidly, processing what the girl just said. "That won't be necessary. You keep it."

Danny and his dad returned to the kitchen in an animated conversation about neckties and white shirts. "Suit fits him like a glove, Martha. But it does need to be pressed."

"Once we have our lists made up, Jane and Danny can drop off her dress, and your suit at the cleaners with instructions that they absolutely must be ready by noon tomorrow."

Satisfied they understood, Martha looked back at the list.

"What to drink? What do you want, Danny? Jane and I are figuring twenty, maybe more what with Tommy and ... Jane, what is your friends name again?"

"Cilla. It's a nickname for Priscilla."

"With Tommy and Cilla calling around," Martha continued.

"I'll order a keg of beer. We won't bother with bottles—plastic cups will do. Maybe two kegs if we can return one ... if we don't need it," Danny said.

"Arnie, I think some bottles of cold drinks—pop, and water maybe."

"After the cleaners, Janie and I are going to the jewelers to pick out our wedding bands."

"Hold on there, son. Martha, what about those two rings in your jewelry case, Danny's great grandfather and great grandmother's? Seems like a nice way to keep the family going don't you think?"

"It's a thought. I'll go get them, see if they fit."

Martha returned with a little red velvet pouch. She loosened the gold drawstring letting the rings fall into her palm. The gold bands gleamed in the sunlight shining through the kitchen window, a gentle breeze from somewhere ruffling the edge of Danny's *To-Do* list.

"Danny, try them on for size." Martha put the two rings in her son's palm. Jane slipped the larger ring on his ring finger, and he slid the smaller one on her finger next to her diamond.

Danny grinned. "Janie, I think you are a petite version of Great Grandma. We'll go to the jeweler and have it sized. If he can't do it by tomorrow noon, we'll leave it—"

"We'll do no such thing," Jane said pulling her fingers from Danny's hand. "At least not until next week. I'll wrap a string around until it fits. I want to be sure I marry you with this ring. We can do that, can't we, Martha?"

Martha's eyes softened. The girl certainly had the right instincts—the phone call and now a Bradley family ring. "I'm sure we can do something so the ring snuggles around your finger, Jane. Check with the jeweler. If he hesitates in the least, you can have it sized later."

Martha tore off a fresh sheet of paper, writing Danny and Jane at the top. Running her fingers down the list she transferred item by item to the clean sheet. She slid the new sheet to her husband to check if he had anything to add. Arnie ran his fingers down the list, then slid the sheet marked Danny and Jane in front of his son.

"Okay, you two, let's get ready for a wedding. Come on Martha. The grocer is first on our list."

"Martha, is it okay if Cilla spends Saturday night with me … here on the farm?"

"Good idea. With all the food preparations tomorrow … and your bridesmaid will want to help you dress. Of course, I will too."

"Of course. I wouldn't want it any other way."

Jane and Danny rushed out the door with the wedding dress in the garment bag and his dad's suit over his arm, and the red velvet pouch in Jane's purse to check with the jeweler. Stopping, Danny rushed back into the house giving his mother a peck on her cheek. "I love you, Mom."

In the truck, Jane took hold of Danny's hand, tapping to get his attention. "Danny, I left a message at my father's office. The women said he wasn't expected until Monday. I told her I was getting married this Sunday."

"I'm sorry, Janie. That must have been hard … do you want to postpone—"

"No. I didn't want you to consider that, but I thought I had to tell you." Jane sighed. "Now, Mr. Bradley, after the cleaners and the jewelers, can we drive to Smithfield Farm, walk through our plans with the manager?"

Danny hit his forehead. "Why didn't I think of that? Of course, and we'll call mom and dad—let them know if there are any changes."

"Great. After Smithfield's it will be late. Can you drop me off at Cilla's? It will be our last night at her house. Kinda fun."

"You bet. One more day, Janie."

Jane looked out the window as they drove up to the cleaners. *One more day!* "Okay if you pick up Cilla and me early tomorrow morning? I'll have my suitcases packed with all my clothes. After the wedding maybe your mom and dad can take her home so she can leave on vacation with her parents as scheduled. Of course, knowing Cilla, she will have hooked a ride with Tommy or one of your other buddies."

Jane turned to Danny stretching to kiss him on the cheek. "Danny, I'm so excited. It's happening. It's really happening. We're getting married."

Chapter 33

———

ORGANIZED OR NOT, chaos reigned supreme in the farmhouse.

Preparations for the wedding dominated all activity. Arnie was dispatched to the grocer early Saturday morning to pick up the items ordered late the day before. On the list were the fixings for the sandwiches—bread, tuna salad, egg salad, slices of smoked ham, slices of cheese—and two decorated sheet cakes.

Long before his dad left, Danny was on his way to pick up Jane and Cilla. Cilla trudged out to BigRed hauling her overnight bag and three dresses – her prom dress for bridesmaid duties plus a casual dress, and a pretty flippy one for Jane to change into after the she-does and he-does vows. The flippy dress was Cilla's idea so the bride could relax, have fun, at the reception without fear of putting Martha's wedding dress in danger of a tear or spill.

Back at the farmhouse Jane, Danny, and Cilla unloaded BigRed at the same time Arnie and Martha returned from the grocer. Martha made a call to the Smithfield Farm manager asking about bowls and platters for serving the food they were bringing. The answer was, yes, they could supply them.

Thrilled at the sight of the cakes, Jane clapped her hands and hugged her bridesmaid. Little bride and groom figures were centered on each cake, circled with *Janie and Danny*, piped in yellow frosting.

Under Martha's direction, Cilla began putting together the sandwiches. Room was made in the kitchen refrigerator, and then the big fridge on the side porch, as the piles of sandwiches grew. Boxes were lined up in the hallway ready to receive whatever had to be transported the next day to Smithfield Farm.

Danny and Jane left. First stop—the cleaners to pick up her gown and his suit, checking there were no spots, smell of cedar was removed, and wrinkles pressed out.

When they returned to the house, Jane tackled the finger sandwiches alongside Cilla. The two girls giggled, twirled between mixing the tuna fish and egg salad. Their spastic actions brought a smile to Martha's lips along with issuing a warning—not too much mayonnaise in the tuna and egg mixes.

Tommy called Danny. Tommy told him not to worry—he had the beer covered. He was picking up the beer kegs, two at the very least.

Sudden hunger pangs hit them all. Martha came to the rescue transferring the current batch of sandwiches to a platter—the little-finger delicacies should be sampled to be sure they were just right for the wedding guests. *Well, didn't they?* Martha thought chuckling.

Arnie was sent yet again to the grocer for paper plates, napkins, and a supply of forks for the cake.

It was almost five o'clock when everyone flopped down at the kitchen table, lists fanned out in front of them. Arnie leaned against Martha watching as she ran her finger down their list, checking off each line item.

Danny mimicked his dad, his arm around Jane's shoulders, leaning in, watching her as she ticked off the items on their list. Cilla sat at the end painting her nails, blowing on them to dry, holding them out in front of her making sure the tomato-red polish was perfect.

Suzy and Dog were under the table ignoring what was going on above them.

Checking off the final item, Martha waited for Jane to finish. With Jane's last stroke, they locked eyes, both smiling. Father and son leaned back and Cilla screwed the nail polish brush in place.

Done!

Silence filled the kitchen.

They had accomplished the impossible.

Dog got up, stretched, whined at the back door to go out. Suzy followed him. Danny rose, stretched, and opened the door for the pooches.

Arnie stood, stretching. "Wine any one?"

"Only if you slice my meatloaf on a platter, while I serve up the roasted potatoes in a bowl. Can't be drinking on an empty stomach ... tired as we all are," Martha said.

After the frenzy of the prior days, everyone moved in slow motion—Jane set the table, Arnie poured the wine, and Martha scraped the sheet pan of potatoes into a bowl handing it to Cilla.

Conversation was sporadic—a comment, chuckles over the frenzy of the past few days, the past week.

After dinner, dishes in the dishwasher, Cilla asked Jane to show her around the farm. She needed some fresh air and a brisk walk to loosen her cramped muscles. Jane introduced her to Daisy, then Sir Charles. Jane polished an apple on her shorts, handed it Cilla to give to Mildred.

Danny tagged along with the girls. He was not letting Jane out of his sight for a minute. He teared up more than once listening to how much Jane had learned in the few days he had been in Portsmouth. It was as if she had been on the farm all her life.

Returning to the house, everyone congregated on the lawn chairs Arnie had set out. It was a beautiful New England summer evening. One not to be missed.

Relaxing as the sun set, they chatted quietly, reflecting on everything that had happened since graduation—lives changing, new paths to follow.

Arnie yawned, apologized—he couldn't help it. He was bone tired.

Jane thanked him and Martha for everything they had done that day, and the days prior. She kissed Danny good night, and then she and Cilla climbed the stairs to the guest bedroom.

It had already been decided not to worry about the bride and groom seeing each other the next day. Given the logistics, that was a tradition to be ignored. But Jane insisted Danny was not going see her in her dress until his father escorted her to his son, placing her hand in his.

• • •

UNBEKNOWNST TO THE HAPPY COUPLE, Tommy was having a whale of a time on the telephone—dialing and receiving calls. Spreading the word that the captain of the football team is marrying Jane O'Neill. "Everyone is invited. Bring a date if you like. A BIG party at Smithfield Farm, in Manchester… you know, the place the prom was held. This Sunday. Tomorrow! Two o'clock sharp."

Tommy made a third dash to the liquor store.

Chapter 34

___

The Wedding

A PERPETUAL GRIN across his face, Danny, pointed BigRed down the driveway. Today he was going to marry the love of his life, a love he vowed would last forever. His mother dressed in her Sunday best, navy blue dress with a lace collar, hands clasped in her lap, sat in the passenger seat gazing out at the passing countryside.

Back at the farmhouse Cilla was helping Jane into her wedding gown—something borrowed along with Martha's pearl-stud earrings. Earrings her mother gave her to wear with the wedding dress. Cilla handed Jane a small gift wrapped in white tissue paper and a blue satin ribbon. Jane giggled with her friend when she opened the package to find a blue garter adorned with a tiny pink bow.

Arnie waited outside by his station wagon—washed and polished. He was transporting his son's bride and bridesmaid to Smithfield Farm. Father like son, Arnie also wore a grin. Two overnight cases were in the back along with a garment bag with outfits the couple could change into after the ceremony, something more casual. Both Jane and Danny, but particularly Jane, were afraid of spilling something on their wedding clothes. Jane had checked for the umpteenth time as she ran up the stairs to dress, asking Arnie to check again to be sure the garment bags were in the car.

• • •

DANNY COCKED HIS HEAD to see better as he turned into Smithfield Farm.

"Holy cow, Mom, look at all the cars."

"Oh, dear. Maybe the people who originally booked the barn had a change of heart ... didn't cancel. But where is everyone?"

Danny helped his mom out of the truck. They strolled up the path, passed a small white-arrow sign stuck in the grass—*Lake.* Cresting the hill, the stillness of the sunlit day was suddenly broken when Danny's high school five-man band, minus one, struck up a raucous rendition of "He's a Jolly Good Fellow." A chorus of over a hundred high-school friends—graduates, current Juniors and Seniors—sang out, shouting the words, Tommy's arms gyrating as he led the musicians.

Beaming, his mom on his arm, Danny passed his friends nodding in recognition as they strolled down to the shores of the lake. Stillness returned after two choruses, the jubilant guests craning their necks watching for the bride.

Hank, the minister, stood under a white canopy erected by the Smithfields, ready to greet the wedding party. In his black suit, white shirt with black cleric collar, Hank smiled as Martha and Danny approached. He kissed Martha's cheek, shook Danny's hand. Tommy dashed up to the trio, taking his position next to Danny, who handed the rings to his best man.

The warm summer air filled again with a rather rocky version of the Lohengrin opera by German composer Richard Wagner, the portion known as *the wedding march*. It was obvious the musicians knew little of the classic piece but they were giving it a good try. It was especially tricky without their leader standing beside the groom.

Cilla crested the hill first in her pink taffeta prom dress, holding a spray of daisies and pink roses. A local florist had delivered two bouquets and a boutonniere to Smithfield Farm that morning. After all, the captain of the football and basketball teams, not to mention a new soldier, deserved a special sendoff.

Several steps behind Cilla the bride emerged on the arm of her future father-in-law. The guests couldn't help themselves letting out a spontaneous whoop—cheering, clapping, fist pumping for the beautiful bride. The transformation from plain Jane to a radiant bride in a silk lace gown was stunning. Jane paid them no mind. Her eyes, brimming with love, were riveted on her groom.

Danny, his heart beating so rapidly it could pop from his chest at the sight of his bride, strode to meet her. Holding out his arm, elbow crooked to receive her hand, he smiled at his dad. "I'll take her from here. Thanks, Dad."

Stepping in front of the smiling minister, Danny whispered in Jane's ear. "You are so beautiful you take my breath away."

Jane smiled up at him and then they both turned to the minister who led them through their vows, the exchanging of rings, joining them as husband and wife. As Danny kissed his bride, Tommy took several Polaroid's of the bride and groom kissing, swiveled and took a couple pictures of the guests. Tommy, a sly smile crossing his face, handed the minister a camera from his pants pocket, showed him the button to press, informing him he was now the designated wedding photographer. Tommy said he was sorry to ask such a favor, but in the midst of picking up the beer and handling all the phone calls, he totally forgot about pictures. The Polaroid pics were for the bride and groom to keep today.

Tommy then bolted up the hill, snatched the trumpet he entrusted to a friend, a trumpet that he had been practicing on diligently, and led the musicians in an upbeat selection of the current hit song, "They Long To Be Close To You" by the Carpenters. The musicians and bride and groom followed their pied-piper to the barn. The young guests followed in line behind Danny's parents.

Stopping at the barn's entrance, Danny and Jane stepped aside letting the singing guests pass with hugs, tears, handshakes. After all the guests passed, the newlyweds entered the barn, paused, their heads swiveling, looking from one side of the barn to the other. Their friends had arrived six hours earlier decorating the barn with white and gold crepe-paper streamers. Silver and gold wedding bells were hanging from the rafters. Tiny white lights encircled floor to ceiling posts. The twinkling white lights, along with the barn's dimmed track lighting, set a mellow romantic mood.

Arnie hustled up to the bride and groom and bridesmaid, garment bags over his arms. He nodded to them to follow him to the restrooms where they could change while Martha, aided by a group of instant helpers, carted in the food.

Returning to the car Martha received her own surprise. Just inside the barn door, two more folding banquet tables had been set up. Tommy and Cilla's friends not only decorated the barn but brought refreshments and three kegs of beer.

Martha flagged Tommy asking him to take the two overnight cases in the station wagon to the cottage, the one on the far end by the lake. Before Arnie left for the wedding with Jane and Cilla, the owner of Smithfield Farm had called with yet more surprises. The cottage was complimentary for the couple's wedding night. They would find a bottle of champagne and a basket of assorted snacks. It was the least they could do. Mrs. Smithfield added that a large group of the couple's friends had taken up a collection, paying for the rental of the barn—their wedding present.

After the first trip with the food, Martha left the rest to the helpers. She returned to help Cilla and her new daughter-in-law. Jane had slipped Martha's wedding gown back in the garment bag, reverently returning the dress to Martha.

"The dress will go back in the cedar chest, Jane. Maybe someday a daughter of yours will wear it."

Jane's mouth gaped open, a gasp of air, she bent forward kissing Martha's cheek which sent a pink flush to Martha's face. "Wouldn't that be wonderful—a third bride to wear your mother's handiwork."

Danny returned his dad's suit in the other garment bag, then took Jane's hand, and after a kiss, gave her hand a tug.

It was party time.

They trio re-emerged—Jane in a green and white polka dot dress with a flippy hemline, Danny in a green golf shirt, tan trousers, followed by Cilla bowing to applause in a navy blue mini-dress, her blonde hair falling freely down her back. All the while, the minister was snapping Tommy's camera, twice requesting more film.

Tommy flashed a few more pictures with the Polaroid making sure there were always two—Danny could take a set with him to boot camp, and Jane could sit a framed picture by her bedside, the rest in a scrapbook or to display around the Bradley farmhouse. Tommy knew the separation tomorrow was going to be hard. It was his way of keeping them together.

Jane and Danny circulated, chatting with their friends, mostly his, his hand holding hers, never letting go. Slowly, as if waking from a dream, they were saying goodbye to their guests, thanking them for everything, but most of all their kind wishes.

As Jane predicted, Tommy offered

to take Cilla home. Cilla gave a tearful goodbye to Jane, holding her in a hug, promising she would be over as soon as she returned from vacation. Tommy hugged Danny and told him he'd drop off the empty kegs.

All the food was eaten. The helpers put Martha's items in the back of Arnie's car along with a small amount of wedding cake covered with plastic wrap. The guests, chatting quietly, exhausted, filed out of the barn, then honking horns as a caravan formed, slowly rolling away from Smithfield Farm.

Arnie gave BigRed's keys to Danny for the morning. When Martha stepped to Jane, giving her a gentle hug, Jane thought she saw a tear but then dismissed it as an illusion.

Waving goodbye to his parents, Danny turned to his bride. "I love you, Mrs. Bradley," he said pressing his lips to hers. Her lips raised to meet his.

"Are we really married?" she whispered.

"Certifiably. Now, let's go check out that cottage." Reaching into his pocket he pulled out a key ring, dangling it before her eyes.

Content to stroll as one to the cottage in silence, they gazed at the beautiful grounds of Smithfield Farm—lush grass carpeting the hill, gently cascading to the edge of the lake, tall pines, squirrels scampering about in the setting sun.

Opening the cottage door, they were greeted with a bouquet of flowers, a split bottle of champagne in a terra-cotta wine cooler alongside two champagne flutes. A small tray of cracker packets, a small brick of cheese, and two apples, were centered on the counter in the kitchenette. Tommy had put their suitcases at the foot of the bed.

Jane opened the note card propped up against the champagne bottle. "Compliments of Smithfield Farm. Thank you for choosing us for your wedding."

"See, Mrs. Bradley, our wedding was meant to be—Smithfield had a cancellation and then we called. Serendipity?"

"Definitely meant to be, Mr. Bradley," Jane said, standing on tiptoe to receive her husband's kiss.

"This champagne will be perfect down by the lake. Okay with you?"

"Perfect," she said picking up the flutes as Danny draped a couple of towels over his arm.

Popping the cork, pouring a little champagne in the flutes, they strolled to the lake where under a canopy they had said their vows. Spreading the towels, they sat on the grass with Danny's arm relaxed around her shoulders, her head resting against his chest.

"So, Mrs. Bradley, a day to remember?"

"Yes, Mr. Bradley, definitely a day to remember."

Shifting, he fished his harmonica out of his pocket, leaned forward playing a melancholy tune. Then, wrapping her in his arms, their lips lingering, tasting each other, tucking her head under his chin, Danny whispered, "I'll cherish this first night with you forever."

Chapter 35

———

JANE OPENED HER EYES, blinking at the brilliance of the sunbeam slicing through a crack in the café curtain rod to the sill, covering the four-over-four window panes. Did yesterday really happen she wondered? Most assuredly it did. Her husband, now husband and lover, was lying beside her, cradling her gently against him.

Events happened so quickly the past few days, she didn't have time to think about making love for the first time. There was only the brief conversation with Cilla. There had been a prick of pain and then an overwhelming feeling of heat as they mated, bodies responding to the urgent need for each other, the love for each other. How was she going to stand watching him leave later today? She wanted more nights like the last—the magic of waking in the morning having shared their love, waking with his arms around her.

Danny had been tender every moment, anticipating the stab of pain she was going to feel, and then slowly bringing her to a place of ecstasy, a place she couldn't breathe her emotions so strong, losing all control of her senses save the desire created with each thrust of his body.

Breathing a quiet sigh of contentment, she felt his arm press against her, his body snuggling ever closer.

"Good morning, Mrs. Bradley."

"Hmm, yes, I was thinking the same thing, Mr. Bradley."

"Would you care for a cup of coffee? I checked the coffeemaker on the counter when I opened the champagne last night. I didn't check the—"

Jane turned to face him. "I have a confession to make."

"Oh, oh. You have a sordid past?"

"The first time I ever drank a cup of coffee was the first morning I went to your farm, very early, to feed the chickens and gather the eggs, and oh, yes, complementing Daisy how good she was to lay such beautiful eggs. Oh, wait. No, that was after my second cup. The first cup was the morning after you asked me to marry you. My mother about fainted."

Danny leisurely sat up, rubbing his eyes. "Good grief. That was your first cup? What did you drink before school?"

"Hot chocolate. But I'm developing a taste for coffee and definitely like the jolt it gives me in the morning."

"Phew, because now that you're my wife, coffee is a mandatory start of the day ... that is unless ... are you okay? Sore? I tried to be careful but your response ... I had a hard time—"

Jane sat up, leaned in for a kiss. "Maybe a little sore ... but nothing I can't handle."

"I love you, Mrs. Bradley," he said gently tapping her nose. "Now, for some coffee. I think there's a packet of cocoa if you'd rather—"

"Not on your life. I'm a farmer's wife, the wife of a very handsome farmer I might add, and I drink what he drinks. There's some cream cheese in the fridge with the bagels. I'll put it out while you start the coffee. No lesson on the best way to do that from you, Farmer Bradley. I'll wait for the pro to show me."

"And who might that be?"

"Your mom, of course. Danny, I love the farm—the animals, the smell of crops growing ... I don't even know what they are yet. And Daisy, Sir Charles. I still can't get over how very kind it was for your mom and dad to invite me to stay in the house with them."

"I was hoping they would come around. When I return we'll have options."

"Like what?"

"Like putting a trailer down by the lake, or build a house of our own on the land. There's a lot of land—over two-hundred acres."

"What did your parents do before you became so strong, old enough to help? How old were you anyway?"

"I was five when Dad let me drive the tractor through the gate when he opened it."

"You were an only child. Martha talked a little, once, about wanting to fill the house with children. She didn't elaborate why you were the only one, just leaving it at female problems. Do you have aunts, uncles?"

"Dad has a sister. She wanted nothing to do with the farm— hard work, hard winters. She lives in New Mexico. Same sort of thing with Dad's brother. Scared of horses, he moved to Oregon, as far away as he could get. That was when breeding and racing horses were lucrative."

"You never said how your dad felt about your being drafted. Couldn't he have claimed a hardship? I thought I read somewhere that farmer's children didn't have to serve."

"I wanted to serve. It's going to be hard on us, and two years will seem like forever, but then I can get help with college. There's so much to learn, new ways of planting. Dad says he's too old to go back to school. Besides, I love our country. I want to fight for her, for a good life with you."

Jane nodded she understood, sipped her coffee. "I'm checking into applying at the University of New Hampshire … part-time. Now that I'm Mrs. Jane Bradley, I want to help with the business end of the farm. I've already looked into courses, and into working part-time in the cafeteria. With my chores at the farm in the morning—"

"I'm going to send you most of my paycheck. After all, my room and board are taken care of." He laughed. "Which reminds me, let's get out those instant, mini-size Polaroid pictures Tommy took. I want one for my wallet, and I know just the one."

Jane leaned over to the counter for her purse, retrieving the pictures. "And just which one do you want?"

"Well, there's the wedding photo Tommy took … you look gorgeous. But…

"But…

"I like the sexy green polka dot dress you changed into. The picture he took when I twirled you around and your dress flared out. The guys at the base are going to be so jealous they don't have someone like you waiting for them back home."

"Home, I like that, "Jane whispered. "And, yes, I'll be waiting for you to return. Then we really start married life together."

Chapter 36

———

BIGRED RUMBLED SLOWLY down the rural road, tall grass alongside swaying in the truck's wake.

Silence filled the cab. Danny held his wife's hand across the console. Two hours and he would be boarding the train for Fort Benning.

He turned into the long driveway at the white sign standing to the left of the entrance, Bradley Horse Farm in large black letters set between two stocky wood posts.

Danny stopped, letting the engine idle. Ducking his head for a better view out the windshield, he squeezed Jane's hand. "This will be ours some day. When mom and dad have had enough of the day-to-day, they will pass the farm to me and you."

Jane hadn't thought of the farm that way. A farmer's wife, yes. But with the enormity of Danny's words sinking in, a gasp escaped her lips. "I'll never be ready. I don't know anything—"

"You're learning. Dad said you are a fast study, a sponge. I like the idea of your taking business courses. I'll picture you sitting in class." Inching the truck up alongside the mailbox, he reached out, grasped the mail, handing it to Jane. Putting the truck in gear he continued up the driveway.

A black sedan pulled in behind BigRed. Danny continued to the house, the black car following, parking alongside.

Martha and Arnie emerged from the house as Danny and Jane climbed out of the truck. Martha waited by the back door watching as Arnie hugged Jane. "Danny, you and Jane go on in. Get your things together. We should leave for the train station soon. I'll see what this man wants."

Danny nodded, reached over the side of the truck for the two overnight cases. Glancing at his dad talking to the stranger, he and Jane entered the house accepting a quick hug from Martha. "When you're ready come on down. I fixed some sandwiches. Put a few extra in a sack for you, Danny, to munch on the train. No telling when you'll eat again."

"Thanks, Mom. We won't be long."

Climbing the stairs, Danny set Jane's overnight case on her bed. Setting his suitcase on the floor, he pulled Jane to him. "Welcome home, Mrs. Bradley." He leaned back looking into her sparkling eyes but this time the sparkles came from the tears she was fighting. "Listen to me, sweetheart."

It was the first time he'd called her sweetheart—soft, warm, tender. She nodded, not trusting her voice, a flood of love flowing through her body.

"We say goodbye here. At the station, quick kisses, laughter, and we say 'see you soon.' Okay with you?"

Jane wove her hands around his neck, bending his head as she stood on tiptoe, kissing him with the warmth of a new wife. "I'll be waiting. I love you."

Danny stepped back, picked up his suitcase and continued to his room. "Stay right there, Janie. It won't take me a second to grab my duffel bag," he called over his shoulder.

Within minutes the pair was down in the living room. His dad was talking to the stranger, Martha standing in the doorway to the foyer. "Like I said, you'll find a dairy farm down the road a couple of miles, but the owner's name is Hopkins not Bernstein. Martha, can you get the phonebook for me? I'll take a look if there's a Bernstein in the area." Looking at the stranger, he added. "It's doubtful. Everyone knows everyone around here and I've never heard the name."

"I'm sorry to have bothered you." The stranger glanced at the painting over the fireplace taking several steps closer. "Is this a

Picasso? I recognize the technique, the subject matter—cubism period."

"To be honest with you, my great grandfather won it in a poker game. He was a character. Even made moonshine. He liked it because he said he saw a scoop, one like we use on the farm to scoop feed from grain bags to feed the animals. To me, it looks like what some call modern art, although I doubt Grandfather Bradley ever heard of modern art."

"When was that, your great grandfather playing poker?"

"Shortly before he died. Around 1880 wasn't it, Martha?"

"Around then. We like the colors—grays, a little aqua I guess you'd say. Since then it's been left right were Arnie's grandfather hung it. I've threatened to put it in the attic."

"Well, it certainly does look nice."

"I don't see any Bernstein in the phonebook," Arnie said handing it back to Martha.

"Thanks for looking. I've taken up enough of your time. Have a nice day." The stranger shook Arnie's hand, shook Martha's hand, and left out the front door.

"Who was that, Dad?" Danny asked.

"Didn't give his name. He was looking for a dairy farm but not the Hopkins's place."

"Come on," Martha said. The sandwiches are out in the kitchen, and then we have to get a move on if you're going to make that train, Danny."

Conversation around the table was light small talk—incidents at the wedding, Daisy laying only one egg this morning. Pushing their chairs back, Martha cleared the dishes with Jane's help, and then joined the men outside by the car.

It wasn't long before they were parked at the train station. As all families before them and probably after, they fought to keep their emotions under control. Arnie caught Martha a few times turning away, hanky in hand, dabbing at something in her eyes.

The locomotive belched.

Danny snatched his duffel.

Shook his dad's hand.

Kissed his mother's cheek.

Gave Jane a quick peck on her perky lips, then another kiss on the perky lips. "See you soon, Janie."

"See you soon, Danny."

A smile pasted on his face, he boarded the train.

The new farmer's wife stood next to her new in-laws, all waving as the train rolled out of the station.

Part III
Chapter 37

———

THE BACK OF ARNIE'S HAND rested on his forehead, eyes fixed on the ceiling. Martha swung her legs up under the sheet blanket, rolled to turn off the bedside lamp, rolled next to her husband. Her husband reached for her hand, kissed the veined skin, then laid their clasped hands back on the blanket.

They heard Jane crying in her room down the hall. From the sounds of it, the girl was trying to stifle the cries, muffled perhaps by a pillow.

Martha, eyes on the ceiling, let out a sigh. "She's just a child. Parents abandoning her, and now her husband of one day leaves."

"Yes, but she has grit. I've seen it in her eyes. Like when she first approached Sir Charles. She was afraid, but reached out her hand holding the apple. As far as she knew, the big horse would bite her hand off, apple and all." Arnie chuckled remembering how the girl, red hair tied back, lifted her head as she stuck out her hand daring the horse, letting him know that she was someone to be reckoned with.

"I worry about our son."

"He's strong, Martha. Strong in body, mind, and character.

"Did you see, feel how he hugged us, Jane? Fear?"

"No. He threw his shoulders back, head high. He has a sense of purpose, fighting for our country. He's leaving us a boy and will come back to his wife a man. Those two will have a good life. And, he knows we'll take good care of her while he's gone."

Martha lifted Arnie's hands. "Hear that?"

"I don't hear anything."

"Jane stopped crying." Martha let their hands drop down on the blanket.

"Good. Now, let's get some sleep."

"Arnie, we have to talk … in the morning. Things happened so fast, you and I haven't had a moment to make plans, how we're going to cope without Danny. We have to figure out how to save the farm. Finances are not good."

"You're right but there are still three of us, four when Danny comes home."

"Did you see the headline in the paper?"

"You mean where President Nixon is trying to apply diplomatic pressure on the Soviets to help encourage the North Vietnamese to engage in serious negotiations? That headline?"

"Yes. It also reiterated that the President was sending Kissinger to China hoping for a breakthrough in our relations with the so-called People's Republic of China *and* the Soviets."

"That will be tricky because he won't want to be accused of being soft on communism."

"Arnie, what is our son walking into?"

Arnie squeezed Martha's hand, turned on his side switching off the lamp beside the bed. Sighing, he laid his head back on the pillow, leaving his wife's question unanswered.

● ● ●

"IT'S THE PAINTING, Vincenzo. I saw it with my own eyes … over the fireplace. I tell you that family knows more than they're admitting. Won it in a poker game my foot. That old Bradley, a shyster, killed Scarpetti, your ancestor, and buried him in the cellar. Scarpetti's bones written up in that newspaper story, were found in that cellar. It was eerie, thinking I was standing on top of where he was buried all these years … close to fifty."

"Well, Frankie, you could be right about that skeleton, could be my Grandfather Scarpetti, but there's no way of telling for sure."

Vincenzo, phone to his ear, looked out the bay window, his mind ruminating over what he had been told over the years. Stories handed down from one generation to the next. Someone in the mob had turned against his brothers and had stolen treasures collected over the years—paintings, gems, and no one knew for sure how many thousands of dollars. If that painting was as Frankie said, then the rest of the treasure could be hidden away on that farm. Horse farm? Racehorses and fast cars? Yes, it fits. It was a known fact in the family that the Bradley patriarch at the time worked for the mob. He suddenly became too busy for mob stuff and just as suddenly had the money to buy thoroughbreds.

"You can at least claim the painting," Frankie said.

"Claim? And just how do you think *I'm* going to claim it? Walk in and say that painting over your fireplace is mine. That your grandfather, or whoever the man said, stole it from my family?"

"No. Claim it like walking in, removing it from the wall, and walking out. Of course, they won't know who took it. I think there are only four living there. The Mr. and Mrs. and two teenage kids. The boy could be twenty."

Chapter 38

———

SIR WINSTON HERALDED the dawning of a new day, notifying the farm that it was time to rise and shine.

Jane slowly dragged her feet from under the blanket and sat on the edge of the bed. Sighing, she rubbed her eyes. Six days since Danny left and she still slept fitfully, dreaming of trains pulling out of railroad stations one after the other. A week since she became Mrs. Daniel Bradley. Her husband was starting life as a soldier and she was starting life as a farmer's wife.

"Farmer's wife." Gazing out the window, her lips turned up in a smile. She liked the sound of it, and all the adventures life on a farm brought each day ... so far anyway.

Soft gray light of dawn filled the room. It was a pretty room. White wainscoting, blue wallpaper with small flowers scattered about in various colors. Cheerful. The room had two windows, both framed with gauzy white Priscilla tiebacks, ruffled on the edges, falling a few inches below the sill. Cilla had explained the origin of the classic curtains, country curtains bearing her name, the night she spent in the room, the night before the wedding.

How did Cilla know about the curtains? I have so much to learn.

Jane turned to the door, closed for privacy but allowing access under the doorframe for the scent of fresh coffee to permeate the air. Jane loved everything so far about the farm, although she still wasn't quite sure she liked the bitter taste of coffee. But, she had to admit she liked the jolt of caffeine. Martha, or was it Arnie, had told her that Danny was given a cup of coffee when he was five.

Sir Winston let out another cock-a-doodle-do, insisting that she get a move on.

Dressing quickly, she hurried down the stairs to the kitchen. Martha was flipping pancakes and Arnie was reading the newspaper.

"Jane, Arnie and I are going to church this morning after the animals are tended to. You're welcome to come with us. What church did you and your parents belong to?" Martha asked setting a platter of pancakes by Arnie. "Our family, since Marshall Bradley bought the farm, have been Congregationalists. How about you?"

"I'd like to go with you. I only went a few times."

Arnie caught Martha's eye, the thought of not attending church on Sunday had never occurred to them. It was the one time Martha had a chance to chat with her friends.

Jane poured a cup of coffee, glanced at Martha. "Anything I can do to help?"

"No. You sit down and have your breakfast. Daisy will wait for you. We'll leave for church at ten. You can meet us outside at the car.

Jane felt a bit awkward without Danny, breakfasts with her in-laws. She felt she had to fill the silence with brilliant conversation ... conversation of some kind.

"My first day of school is tomorrow. But don't worry I'll take care of the chickens. I already got a job in the cafeteria busing dishes on the days I'm on campus."

"What days would that be?" Martha asked.

"Monday and Tuesday. I should be back home ... here, by two ... after the school's lunchtime. On Wednesday, I look forward to helping out more on the farm. Please give me more chores besides the chickens. And, Martha, please, please teach me how to cook like you. How to garden, how to put up jellies, jams, how to can tomatoes—"

"Wow, that's quite a list. Tell us about your classes. What are you taking, Jane?" Arnie asked.

"It's a summer class, Business Accounting 101. Martha, I may have some questions for you, you know, about what the textbook says to do as opposed to how it works for you in the real world."

"I never had any schooling. I'm sure I won't know what you're talking about."

"Martha, that's not true. You've kept the farm's books ever since my mother turned them over to you many years ago."

Hastily eating the remaining pancake, washing it down with the last drop of coffee, Jane put her dishes in the sink anxious to leave the tension-filled air. "I'll be ready, ten o'clock. Thanks for breakfast, Martha."

● ● ●

THE WHITE CLAPBOARD CHURCH sat at the top of a slight rise. Off to the side was a cemetery. Slabs of slate or granite marked the graves of those who passed. Buttercups dotted the landscape around the church, around the markers, and down to the old rock wall, rocks of various sizes piled one on the other holding the embankment from the road.

Hands in her lap, Jane leaned forward in the car to take a mental image of where Danny had gone to church. He hadn't spoken of the little church with the bell tower piercing the sky.

Arnie parked the car next to the last in line that had just pulled in, forming a jagged row. Nodding to friends as they got out of the car, Martha led the way to the entrance, large double doors of weather-beaten oak.

Stepping inside, Martha strode down the red carpet to a pew on the left, sliding in on the gleaming oak. Arnie nodded to Jane to sit next to Martha and then he settled next to her. Jane was enchanted by the stark white interior warmed by the burnished oak trim around Palladian windows. A row of golden pipes rose behind the altar to the peak of the vaulted ceiling. Clear glass panes provided a view of the thick vegetation of century-old trees and recent bushes, some filled with shades of pink flowers. Hanging brass fixtures with a spray of five frosted glass shades providing a soft glow from the light bulbs inside.

Jane's eyes dropped to her lap, glancing left and right at her in-laws, watching, ready to follow what they did. She felt a calm sweep over her in the quiet atmosphere, hearing greetings whispered by the parishioners, one to the other, as they took their seats.

The minister entered, gave a short prayer, then everyone stood as the organist filled the church with rising and falling chords, music flowing from the golden pipes. Arnie handed Jane a hymnal, Martha held her hymnal open, pointing to the number. Jane mouthed the words, hesitant to make a sound until she whispered the final amen with the congregation.

Filing out on the red carpet to the brilliance of the sun-filled morning, Arnie and Martha stopped, greeted by the minister. Arnie introduced Jane, saying that she was Danny's bride, and that Danny had left last week for boot camp at Fort Benning.

During the drive back to the farm, Arnie and Martha chatted quietly in the front seat. Once Arnie looked in the rearview mirror at Jane. "How did you like going to church, Jane?"

Jane leaned forward between the seats answering with a bright smile. "I enjoyed it … everything. The church is beautiful and I liked the minister's message. Are there Bradley relatives in the cemetery?"

"No. There's a family plot on the farm, by the lake. Maybe someday when you're at the horse barn, we can stroll to the group of plots. I can give you some more history of the family you married into."

"I'd like that." Jane leaned back in her seat. Looking at the rings on her finger, she suddenly felt at peace coupled with a sense of anxiousness to get on with her new life. School tomorrow. She had plans to learn more about the farm by asking for examples from Martha, as she did her accounting homework.

Turning into their long driveway, Arnie parked in his usual spot. As Martha eased out of the car she darted to the back door, calling over her shoulder that the phone was ringing.

"Hello. Hello. Danny?"

"Hi, Mom. Yes, it's Private Daniel Bradley."

"We just got home from church ... here's your father."

"Hello, son. How is it going so far?"

"So far so good. Is Janie there?"

"She sure is. Jane, it's Danny. I think he wants to talk to his wife," Arnie said grinning as he handed the receiver to her.

Jane turned her back to her in-laws as she clutched the phone to her ear. "Danny?" she whispered, a tear spilling over her lid.

"I miss you, Janie ... miss you, sweetheart. I wrote a letter to you this morning. They shaved my head, called it an induction cut. I look like a goat, shaved to the skin. I'll send you a picture if you promise not to laugh."

"I won't laugh, Danny. I went to church with your parents this morning."

"How did that go?"

"Nice. Your dad said maybe next Sunday, if there's time, he'll show me the family plot on the farm, give me a history lesson—stories about your ancestors. How is it, Danny, the Army?"

"Not bad. I was assigned a barrack with some other guys. Don't know any of them. I play my harmonica most nights until lights out. The guys keep asking me to play different songs. Good thing I had that high school band. I remembered most of the pieces ... or they hummed the notes, close enough. We get up at 4:30 in the morning. Some of the guys groan, complain. But heck, for me it's like another day at the farm with Daisy and Sir Charles."

Danny's voice was strained. Jane knew he was putting on a brave face for her. She struggled to stop the tears, keeping the same brave face thing for him.

"I miss you, Janie ... miss you, sweetheart. I'll keep writing."

"I miss you too, Danny, with every breath. I love you."

"Bye, Janie."

Jane clutched the receiver. As long as she hung on she felt he was still there.

"ARNOLD!" Martha's voice was strange, strangling in her throat.

Arnie rushed to the living room. "What's the matter ...

Martha stood in front of the fireplace pointing to the painting, or rather to a rectangle outlined on the wall where the painting had hung for decades.

"Anything else missing?" Arnie asked, his eyes darting around, taking inventory of the room.

"What's the matter—" Jane stopped mid sentence ... the painting was gone.

"Arnie, that man, last week. Maybe he wasn't lost, wasn't stopping for directions."

"Hmm. Thinking back he took an interest in the painting, almost the minute he walked into the room."

Martha looked away from the wall to her husband. "You don't suppose ...

"I don't know. He didn't give his name and we didn't ask. All we know is what he looks like and that he was driving a black car. You and Jane check all the rooms. Go together. Stay together. Yell if you see anything out of place. I'll call the chief." Arnie turned heading to the kitchen phone, calling over his shoulder. "Next time Danny calls, or we write to him, don't mention the painting. He has enough going on without worrying about us."

Chapter 39

———

"GOOD MORNING, SIR WINSTON. I have a very demanding day today. I'm going to school." Scooping the feed into the rubber bowl, refreshing the water, Jane then headed inside the coop to gather the eggs. "Miss Daisy, you've been busy. Three eggs. I hope my day is as productive. I'm wearing a dress, navy blue. What do you think, Miss Daisy?" Miss Daisy's beak jerked one way then the other. "Glad you agree."

Latching the gate on the chickens' playground, and with a skip in her step, Jane hustled up to the house with the basket of eggs. Setting them on the counter, pouring a cup of coffee, she dashed out the back door to BigRed.

Checking the side mirrors and the rearview, Jane turned north on Route 108 to Durham, her mind reviewing the notes she jotted the night before. She had listed questions pertaining to her first class, Introduction to Financial Accounting, and questions to ask the cafeteria manager—was there a dress code, hours she could work after her class. Questions for the bursar about payment for her class. She planned to pay off the four-credit course in three chunks if possible. She wished she could take two courses at a time, but she didn't dare. What if it was too hard and she failed. Better to wait. Take the course then decide how to proceed with her very limited funds. There was the scholarship she received at graduation only a few weeks ago, but now seemed like a lifetime.

She also wanted to check if she was eligible for any discounts on campus. Because of her grades, did she qualify for a student loan?

Then there was the textbook—she added the campus bookstore to her list of stops. A used book would be fine and cheaper. She hoped to show Martha the book, get her help as to how the course related to the farm. Maybe her mother-in-law would warm up a little more when she saw she was trying to be a good farmer's wife for Danny. The ice was thawing, but Martha was still chilly most of the time.

Danny said he was going to send her money but she didn't want to spend it. She wanted to save it, surprise him with a nest egg in a bank account when he returned. Show him she could do her part.

The day she enrolled, she had asked for directions to the building and classroom. Scoping out the campus, she had driven to the mammoth multi-story building.

Today, a thrill raced through her veins as she walked, head held high, to her classroom. The thrill didn't diminish as the professor explained what the class would cover—fundamental concepts of accounting with emphasis on the recording of economic transactions, and the preparation and analysis of financial statements.

Whew, that was heavy, she thought, her head spinning as she joined the other students exiting the classroom. She headed to the cafeteria. Her timing was perfect.

"Hello, Mrs. Adams. Remember me? Jane O'Neill? I was married since I applied to work in the cafeteria. My name is now Mrs. Jane Bradley."

Mrs. Adams grabbed a black three-ring binder leaning against the inside of her desk next to her feet. Her forehead drew into furrows, her mouth shut tight in a frown. Opening the notebook, she flipped to a tab, her finger running down a list of names. Looking up at the woman standing in front of her, she shut the notebook. "I'm sorry, Miss O'Neill, Mrs. Bradley, but that position has been filled with another student, last week. I tried to reach you but the phone was disconnected."

"My parents were moving to California. I never thought about the phone number. Mrs. Adams, I need the job. I'm a good worker—"

"I'm sorry, Jane. But if you have a new number, note it next to your name, with your new name." Mrs. Adams handed the binder to Jane, her index finger pointing to O'Neill. "Please excuse me, I have to check that the lunch service starts without a hitch. First day of classes is always a bit chaotic."

Mrs. Adams rushed past Jane, disappearing into the hall, passed chattering students queuing up with their trays, meaningless chatter filling the void enveloping Jane.

• • •

DRIVING BACK TO THE FARM, disappointment flooded away the earlier excitement of her class. Parking BigRed, she dropped the keys into her tote and walked with sluggish steps into the house.

Arnie was seated at the table, raising a spoon of tomato soup to his mouth. "Jane, you look like you just lost your best friend. School didn't go well?"

Out of the corner of her eye Jane caught Martha's stern face. "Class was great, but I did have a major disappointment. The job at the cafeteria was given to another student. Seems Mrs. Adams tried to reach me but, of course, my parents had disconnected the phone. I didn't think to call to confirm —"

"Always confirm important appointments, Jane. If you had, you could have given this Mrs. Adams our number. She didn't know you were married either, did she?"

"No, she didn't know I was married. I guess I really goofed up."

"Chalk it up to one of life's lessons. It won't be the last," Arnie said with a chuckle. "Don't you fret. Something else will come along. Now sit, have some of Martha's tomato soup. You'll feel better and we want to hear about your class, don't we, Martha?"

"I'm not really hungry."

"That's silly. You haven't had anything but a cup of coffee this morning, that I know of," he added. "The chief dropped by. No lead on who stole our painting, but he suggests we keep the doors locked from here on when we leave the ..." He stopped, sighed. "Changing times. Never had to lock our doors before. I had a set of keys made for you—one for the front and one for the back. He also said there was nothing new on the skeleton. Goody had been very busy—no information on the age of the bones."

Chapter 40

———

"JANE, THERE'S A LETTER for you from Danny ... on the kitchen counter. Must be long because it's heavier than usual," Martha called out from her office.

Putting her books on the chair by the stairs, her tote leaning against the chair legs, Jane sprinted to the kitchen, snatching the letter leaning against the pepper shaker. They had exchanged several letters, days apart, mostly filled with their daily routine. Jane kept them in the drawer of her nightstand, rereading at least one or two every night.

Looking up at Martha with a growing grin, Jane slit the envelope open. Pulling out two sheets of paper and a photo, she plopped down on a kitchen chair.

Martha strode out the back door looking for Arnie. He was down the path a ways walking toward her. Martha waved at him to hurry. "Jane has a letter from Danny," she shouted.

Arnie quickened his stride, joining his wife and Jane in the kitchen. "What does he say, Jane?"

"Well, first of all there is a note card for you, a picture of Danny, and a letter for me." Jane handed the card, and the picture of Danny, standing with some other soldiers at the main gate of the fort, to Martha.

"Read yours first, Jane," Arnie said.

"Okay." She hesitated a split second wondering if there was something too personal, but it had been awhile since they'd had a

letter, more than two weeks, so she unfolded the sheet and read
it out loud.

> July 2
>
> Dearest Janie,
>
> Here's a picture of me and my buddies, all with fuzz on our
> heads compliments of the Army's barber.
>
> Days are long and physically challenging.
>
> Just before lights out, the guys gather around my bunk and
> I play my harmonica. Usually something lively but always
> ending with a love song. One of the guys has a great voice. He
> sings the last song while I accompany him.
>
> Keep writing about your days—school, the farm, all you
> are learning on both fronts.
>
> Give a warm greeting to Daisy and Sir Winston. Watch out
> they don't peck your fingers.
>
> I still hold close the sound of your voice when I first called
> from the base. I love you, Mrs. Bradley.
>
> See you in a little while.
>
> Your husband,
>
> Danny.

She sighed, a wistful look on her face. "Okay, now it's your
turn. What does the card say?"

Arnie held the card out so he could see better, pushing his
reading glasses up higher on his nose. "Here goes."

> July 2
>
> Hi, Mom and Dad. I'm doing just fine and really like my
> new friends. Who would have thought all those times
> tinkering with tractors, thrashers, and BigRed, I was actually
> training for the Army.
>
> Now that I've been assigned to the armored tank division,
> maintenance of the equipment, the guys assigned with me
> and I are pouring over maintenance manuals, learning all we

can to keep our guys on the battlefield armed with the best stuff that works.

The scuttlebutt is that we'll be deploying around mid-September. Of course, that's subject to change.

Less than two years I'll be home and eligible to take courses on the GI Bill—learn some new tricks and the latest in farming, land management.

Love, your son
Danny.

Chapter 41

———

JANE RACED DOWN THE DRIVEWAY. The mail carrier had just stopped, slipping what she thought was a letter in the box. Martha and Arnie had gone to the store, so she could read her letter in private, if there was a letter. It had been a month since she received the last one and it was now the last week of August.

There was a letter on top of a fistful of junk mail. Her only thought was to rip the envelope open. She flopped down on the grass, leaned against the Bradley sign, and did just that—slit the flap with her fingernail.

• • •

AUGUST 9

Hi sweetheart,

I showed all the guys the picture you sent feeding the chickens, holding up one of Daisy's eggs. They didn't comment on the egg because they were too busy passing the picture around and asking how did I snag such a pretty woman.

Yes, I'm still playing the harmonica every night. The GIs gather round, sometimes singing, other times a melancholy song will make them think of the girls back home and they just listen.

As you have probably guessed, I've been deployed—about two weeks ago. Our letters will take longer to reach each other. I can't say where we are only that I miss you.

My squad is kept busy maintaining the vehicles. As soon as we patch them up they're driven back to the front. I started marking them—one of the jeeps left the maintenance shed in the morning and was back that night— different driver.

Sorry, I just got notice that more vehicles are due to arrive momentarily so I'll sign off.

Miss you bad.

Love,

Danny.

• • •

AUGUST 21

Dear Danny,

Your letter just arrived. It took two weeks. I sat on the grass by the farm's sign. Couldn't wait to read it. Miss you bad too!!

I received my grade for my first class—A. How about that? *That* means, so far, I am a straight-A student. My final was nerve racking even though I studied like crazy. Your mom even helped me review the chapters and my notes. She said she was learning too. She actually shared with me her record-keeping sheets for the farm.

I signed up for the next business class, starts the day after Labor Day. New class. New month. You know in the movies where pages on a calendar flip like they're caught in the wind? That's how I feel sometimes, but most times it seems like forever since you left and even longer until you return.

Anyway, the next class is intro to statistics. There's even a lab. Don't I sound brainy? Quote: The use of statistical methods for managerial decision making. End quote. The professor told the class we will learn problem solving strategies. Martha laughed. Her strategy is to keep the new baby pigs fed so they can be sold fat and sassy. Yes, she and your dad decided to raise pigs! The piglets are cute but I think they'll be scary when they get big.

Your checks are coming in the mail. Thanks. I'm putting ninety percent of the money in our savings account. I opened one in both of our names but you have to sign a card before you can withdraw funds. Should I send the card in the mail? Is it safe for you to mail it back to me? What do you suggest?

During the break between my classes, your mom and dad gave me some new chores—feeding the pigs and Sir Charles along with the chickens. They all seem to know me ... scamper to me. Sir Charles whinnies. I know what you're thinking ... they just want to be fed.

Well, I'd better turn out the light. You know, a farmer's wife is up and at 'em when the rooster calls.

I miss you every minute. Please, please, take care of yourself.

All my love,
Janie

• • •

JANE LICKED THE ENVELOPE, sealed it, and stood it next to the lamp, ready to put it in the mailbox for tomorrow's pickup. Turning out the bedside lamp, she snuggled under the coverlet. The nights were still warm but Martha had laid a folded quilt at the foot of her bed. It was a beautiful quilt. She said Danny's grandmother appliquéd the baskets of flowers, and quilted the batting inside with a group of friends—a quilting bee.

Jane didn't include in her letter that, from what she saw of the books, the farm was not doing well at all. It needed a dose of what she was learning in her class—decision making strategies.

Her thoughts filled with Danny. They always drifted to Danny, no matter what she was doing, no matter where she was.

The family watched the news every night. If news from the war came on during the day Arnie turned it off. He said a nightly update was all they needed.

Jane knew he watched the war reports on the little television in the barn. He simply didn't want to alarm her and Martha with the non-stop commentary. Last night the reporter said the war effort didn't look good. There were rumors that morale among the troops, and their family's back home, was ebbing.

Chapter 42

———

AHEAD OF SIR WINSTON'S call for a new day, Jane threw off the covers making a mad dash to the bathroom—vomit erupting from her stomach. Retching continued as she slumped to her knees, gripping the sides of the white porcelain toilet bowl.

She was aware that Martha was kneeling beside her, holding a cold wet washcloth to her forehead. Jane struggled to speak between retches. "Must have been … the fish at the cafeteria … after orientation. Tasted off."

"Breathe deep, Jane. Here, take a sip of water." Martha held a glass to Jane's lips.

Gulping air between sips, her stomach seemed to settle.

Daring to move, Jane pushed away from the toilet, Martha flushed away the remains of Jane's stomach, helping her to her feet. She stood a moment. "I'm okay, I think. It came on so suddenly."

"Take a shower and come on down for breakfast," Martha said hanging the washcloth over the towel bar.

"Okay. Maybe just a piece of toast, coffee. I have school today. I have to go, first day of the semester. But I tell you, I sure won't eat lunch in the cafeteria."

The shower seemed to perk her up and her appetite along with it, but she wasn't going to take any chances—toast and coffee would be it for breakfast.

Arnie was already down in the horse barn when Jane entered the kitchen. Martha nodded that the two slices of toast were hers as she poured the coffee.

"I asked Arnie to take over your chores this morning. Said you weren't feeling well."

"Okay ... probably best."

"I'm going in for groceries this morning, Jane. Anything you want me to pick up?"

"No, and thanks for your help ... upstairs. I'm a bit shaky ... but no nausea. I'll be fine at school."

"A stomach bug can hit hard. If you feel the least bit sick at school, you come on home."

"I will. I'll take my coffee with me. Thanks for the toast. See you this afternoon," Jane called out as she left.

Martha looked out the window at BigRed's taillights receding down the driveway.

"Jane's running a bit late?" Arnie asked as he padded in the back door, slumping on a chair.

"A little. I'm going to the grocery. Anything I can get for you?"

"Yeah, some antacid. Took the last one this morning."

Martha turned, took stock of her husband. Maybe there was a bug in the house. Well, she was going to find out, a process of elimination. Tidying up the kitchen, she pushed the button on the dishwasher, tore the list of grocery items off the pad attached to the refrigerator, picked up her purse and car keys on the table in the foyer. Within an hour of Jane's departure she was turning out of the driveway on her way to the grocer and the drugstore. She made a mental note of a phone call she was going to make after her errands were completed.

● ● ●

RETURNING HOME AT HER normal time after school, Jane immediately headed up the stairs to change into jeans ready to tackle her chores. Arnie said he was starting to harvest the hay for winter today. He'd hired a part-time helper and she was welcome to join them.

Martha knocked on the doorframe of Jane's bedroom just as she was pulling up her jeans. "How are you feeling?"

"Okay, tired ... a little. I think all that's happened caught up with me this morning."

"I made an appointment for this afternoon ... for you."

Jane pulled up the zipper on her jeans. "Would you look at that ... I can't hook the button. Your cooking is just too good." Jane glanced at Martha. She had a funny look on her face. "What kind of appointment?"

"With my doctor, my woman doctor. You don't have to go. I can cancel it."

"Why with your woman doctor?"

"Jane ... you may be pregnant ..."

Jane laughed. "Martha, that can't be possible ... my wedding night?"

"I had several miscarriages ... you've gone through a lot. You might be right, on the other hand, if you are ... you have to take care of yourself."

Jane could see the worry lines deepen on Martha's face, more than that, she looked concerned bordering on frightened. If she didn't keep the appointment it would look like she was being disrespectful to her mother-in-law, not taking seriously the pain she had gone through, and she certainly didn't want to do that after what Martha had done for her.

"It's okay, Martha. If you think I should see your doctor, then, of course, I'll go."

● ● ●

MARTHA WAITED, sitting on the edge of the couch in the doctor's waiting room. Hearing the door open, she looked up as her doctor, grinning, walked up with her new patient, Jane's eyes wide in disbelief, amazement.

"Well, Martha, looks like a new little Bradley is on the way. Congratulations."

Jane shook her head. "It's not possible ... I checked the calendar—"

Martha smiled. "A baby in the house again. It's good news, Jane." Martha rose, arms stretched out, giving her daughter-in-law a warm embrace.

A slight smile on Jane's lips, spread to a wide grin. *A baby, Danny's baby.* The wonder of it filled her heart.

Martha thanked the doctor as the nurse strolled over to Jane with a handful of pamphlets, a date for her next appointment on a card, and instructions on the vitamins she should begin taking.

Jane was speechless. She could only nod to the nurse that she understood.

Martha again thanked the doctor and the nurse, and then guided Jane out the door. The girl was obviously in shock over the news. In Martha's mind—a miracle.

● ● ●

MARTHA'S HUG AND OBVIOUS elation were almost as unexpected as learning she was pregnant. Jane stood in front of the full-length oval mirror from the attic. After seeing her reflection in Martha's wedding dress, she had asked Danny to bring it down to her room, feeling it brought good luck. She turned sideways, hands splayed across her belly. Maybe the doctor was wrong. She didn't see a bulge, or, was there? Her T-shirt was a bit tight. Looking square into the mirror there was a bulge all right. And, her breasts were definitely bigger.

Thoughts tumbling through her head, she shared her thoughts with her reflection. "Danny. I have to write ... I wish I could call. Maybe he won't be happy. But we talked about having scads of kids. Oh my God, he won't be with me when I have the baby. I have to call my parents. They won't be happy, that's for sure ... but perhaps with a grandchild on the way ... grandchild? Oh my God, I sound so old."

● ● ●

JANE DIDN'T KNOW what to do except to go ahead and find Arnie in the hayfield. Dashing down the path, slowing to a fast walk, she waited for him to climb off the tractor, then she marched up to him, flinging her arms around him. She stepped back, her eyes dancing. "Have you seen Martha in the last fifteen minutes?"

"No, Should I have?"

Oh, oh. Maybe I should let Martha tell him. "I'm going to have a baby."

"No fooling?" Arnie's grin slowly spread from ear to ear. "You sure?"

"Martha made an appointment with her doctor. We just got back. The doctor said I was … so I'm sure. What's Danny going to say?"

"I think he'll let out a whoop and holler, little lady."

After a hug, then holding her at arm's length, scrutinizing her tip to toe, he smiled along with another hug.

Arnie insisted he and the farmhand were doing just fine and suggested she help Martha with dinner, or do some homework. She could help with the haying some other time.

At dinner, the three sat at the table, grins darting between them as they passed the platter of meatloaf slices, carrots and chunks of potatoes nestled alongside. For the first time since Jane had shared a meal with the family, Martha said grace. She thanked the Lord for their food, and, oh yes, for a baby coming into the house again.

Then conversation erupted—how to tell Danny the good news. It was decided he should know as soon as possible. Jane would write a letter tonight and stop at the post office on her way to school in the morning. If she had another bout of morning sickness Arnie said he'd post the letter.

Chatter continued—which room for a nursery, and wasn't Danny's pine cradle in the attic, the cradle that all Bradley babies slept in when they were first born, the one with the hood.

• • •

MARTHA AND ARNIE turned off the bedside lamps, both rolling back on their pillows staring at the ceiling.

Arnie let out a sigh. "Jane, Danny's Jane, having a baby."

"She's just a baby herself, Arnie."

"You were only a year older than Jane when you …

"It's okay. You can say it. A year older than Jane when I had my first miscarriage." Martha turned her head on the pillow looking at her husband, worry lines furrowing her forehead.

"Now, now, Martha. Jane will have this baby, a healthy baby. I just know it. I'd like to see Danny's face when he gets her letter. I wish she could call … but he's overseas and … well, if I know our son, he'll figure a way to call us as soon as he reads the letter."

Chapter 43

———

SEPTEMBER 9

My dear, dear Danny,

I have the most amazing news.

Remember when we talked about filling the house with kids? Well, hold on—sit down—number one is on the way?

I certainly am going to have to watch out for you. You must be very virile—our wedding night and we conceive a baby? Wow!

Your mom was beyond kind. I woke up this morning sick, sick, sick. That part of the day was not good. I thought for sure it was the fish I had at the cafeteria after orientation that made me so sick. I made it through the first day, toughed it out even though my stomach was still a bit queasy.

When I got back to the farm that afternoon after my class, your mom had made an appointment with her doctor. She said if I didn't want to go she would cancel it, but she suspected I might be pregnant. I thought no way was I pregnant but I could see she was worried so I went.

I was a little late but never gave it a thought. I mean … our wedding night? As you said at the time—definitely a night to remember.

Your dad is very excited. Gave me a big bear hug. I know your mom is excited too. She's still a bit reserved, never quite lets her guard down but always respectful, but I could see it in her eyes.

Danny, you're going to be a daddy. Can you believe it?

Hope this finds you well. I pray for your safety every night.

With all my love, your wife and baby waiting to be born,

Janie

• • •

SEPTEMBER 9

Dear son,

I'm sure you've read Jane's letter and learned about her big news. Your mother and I are very happy about the pending arrival of a little Bradley.

Danny, rest assured that we will take care of your wife and baby. Martha is already chattering about how we can renovate the house so that your little family will have your own space.

She's thinking a kitchenette, a door between the formal living room and the family room—family room on your side. Kitchenette because she hopes you will join us in the big kitchen more often than not.

Your mother is also talking about the women's guild at church knitting baby clothes, and quilting patches of material together for little blankets.

Your mom goes on and on about how much she is learning from Jane as they tackle Jane's homework together.

We love you, son, and don't worry. Your wife is in loving hands.

Love, Dad

Chapter 44

———

THE WEATHER HAD TURNED cold overnight, as dark gray storm clouds gathered. Stepping out the church doors, Arnie popped a big black umbrella holding it over Martha and Jane.

"You girls wait here. I'll bring the car around," Arnie said turning his jacket collar up, making a run for it.

Picking up the girls, as he had taken to calling them, he drove away from the church heading back to the farm. He was a happy man having his girls with him.

"That was nice, the pastor including a prayer for you, Jane, during the service," Arnie said looking at Jane in the rearview mirror.

"Yes, it was."

"Have you called your parents? Do they know you're carrying their grandchild?" Martha asked. She was sitting in the front seat and didn't see Jane's reaction to her question—the clenching of her fists, the deep inhale of air.

"No ... not yet. I was going to write but then thought it was better to call. Their last letter ... let's see that's two in five months. Anyway, in their last letter they said that I should move to California to wait for Danny. He could join me there. They were sure he could get a job."

Martha sent a sideways look at Arnie. "I see. Did you write back?"

"No. What's the point? But with a baby ...

"How about your girlfriend Cilla?"

"I called the number she gave me for her dorm room at Michigan State. No one answered. I could call her parents, but I'd rather tell her myself about the baby. I wonder if Danny's received our letters? It's been over a month—October already."

"If not, he will soon, dear."

Jane smiled, looking out at the rain pelting what was left of the colorful leaves. Fall was beginning to fade. It was the first time Martha had called her dear. Jane welcomed the warmth of her words, especially after talking about her parents.

Arnie turned up the farm's driveway and parked. He darted to unlock the back door to the ringing of the telephone. Martha rushed by him, snatching the receiver from the wall cradle, a warm feeling running up her arm.

"Danny, Danny, is that you?"

"Yeah, Mom. Sorry the connection's a little scratchy. I just read Jane's letter. A baby, Mom! A baby! Is Janie there?"

"Hold on, son. She's right here and congratulations."

"Danny, did you get my letter?"

"I sure did. Are you all right? How do you feel? Still getting sick?"

Jane chuckled. "I feel wonderful. Considering I'm going to have our baby, I can put up with the morning sickness, but it's subsiding."

"Did you see a doctor yet?"

"Yes. A woman doctor. I like her so much. Your mom suggested her and went with me. I'm very healthy. That's what the doctor said. She gave me some pamphlets on what I can expect and also suggested a few books in the library. Speaking of library, with my school books and the library books I check out, I look like a real scholar. How are you? Everything going well?"

"As well as can be expected. When do you see the doctor again?"

"Four weeks. Call me if you can. I'll send you the exact date."

"Did she give you a list of vitamins? I know with the animals, they have to have vitamins to keep strong … healthy."

"Yes, she did ... Danny, what was that noise? Sounded like a plane."

"Yeah, a few fly overhead from time to time. Nothing to worry about."

"Do you still play your harmonica?"

"Sure do. When I get home I'll play for you and the baby. God, Janie, we're going to have a baby. I wish I could be with you ...

"Your mom and dad are taking very good care of me."

"I have to go, Janie. Keep writing. I wait every day for mail call to see if there's a letter from you. We're moving around a lot ... takes time for the mail to catch up with us. Take care of yourself ... and the little Bradley."

"I will. Stay safe, Danny. We love you."

Chapter 45

———

CLASS WAS EXHILARATING and painful. Jane fully understood what the professor was saying about analyzing profit and loss of a business. From the moment the professor stepped to the chalkboard Jane could see a correlation between what was happening at the farm and the extent of the trouble they were facing.

Turning into the driveway she almost nicked a scruffy looking man—very thin, hair tied together in a ponytail, deep olive skin. He was standing on the edge of the pavement gazing up at the farmhouse. The man was holding a wicker basket by the handle.

Out in the field Arnie had seen him, too, and was walking to the man as Jane slowed to a stop. Normally she would have driven on up to the house, but there was something about the man that drew her to him, maybe it was the way he carefully transferred the basket from one hand to the other so he could hold out his right hand to Arnie.

Arnie shook the man's hand in greeting, exchanging names as Dog darted down the driveway plunking his hind end in front of the man. Whining, Dog poked his wet black nose against the basket.

"Jane, this is Mr. Wolf. He wondered if we could spare a cup of milk for his baby."

"Baby? Where?"

Mr. Wolf set the basket on the ground and gently lifted a soft white piece of blanket revealing a baby with creamy brown skin and big brown eyes, kicking at the intrusion.

"Mr. Bradley, I'm sorry to trouble you. I saw your sign, Bradley Horse Farm, the nice house at the top of the rise. I'm strong. I can work to pay for the milk."

Arnie glanced at Jane who looked to Mr. Wolf, then at the basket. "Mind if I pick her up?" Jane asked, dropping to her knees on the grassy strip next to the pavement.

"It's okay, ma'am. The baby is a boy," he said with a pr
oud grin.

Jane fished her hands under the infant, lifting him to her shoulder. The baby's lips quivered ready to cry out in protest as he was plucked from the warmth of his little bed.

"There, there. It's all right little guy. Your daddy says you're hungry. I think we can help him, can't we Arnie?"

"I don't see why not. Come with us, Mr. Wolf ... what's your first name?"

"Just call me Wolfe, sir, with an E. My mama never used my first name so I don't either."

Dog ran ahead, then back to his family and the visitor, making sure they were still headed up the driveway, Jane leaving BigRed in the middle of the pavement.

"Nice dog. Friendly?" Wolfe asked.

"I'd say you are already one of his new best friends. You looking for a job?"

"Yes, Mr. Bradley."

"What kind of work do you do?"

"Anything you need doing—I've worked on a farm, so I know my way around machines and I do carpentry."

Jane's mind was factoring in the stranger on the cost analysis she was starting. It sounded like he would work for food to begin with, and if he worked out ... well ... maybe she was getting ahead of herself. On the other hand, with Danny gone for awhile and her expecting a baby, they could use more hands to work the farm.

Entering the house, Jane carrying a baby and a scruffy visitor on her heels, then Arnie at the end of the line, Martha wasn't sure what to do. However, no one seemed alarmed and Dog wasn't about to leave Jane alone with the baby or was it he wouldn't leave the baby alone with Jane? Suzy laid in the corner, her big brown eyes darting from one human to the other.

"I have a bottle here in the basket," Wolfe said.

"Wolfe, meet my wife Martha. Martha, this is Mr. Wolfe—"

"Pleased to meet you, Mrs. Bradley. Just call me Wolfe. Can I rinse the bottle out?"

"Certainly, Mr. Wolfe. I'll warm the milk—"

"If it's not too much trouble that would be nice but he can take it either way. I don't want to bother you more than I have."

"I hope you don't mind my asking," Jane said. "Where is your wife, the baby's mother?"

Wolfe turned his pain-filled eyes away. "She died. Complications with our baby's birth."

Jane stared at him a second, her hand covering her mouth. She felt horrible for asking about his wife never expecting him to say she was dead. Her brows scrunched together. She had more questions. "How old is your son … and … what's his name?" Jane's head twisted from Martha to Arnie to Wolfe.

"He's four months. We, my wife and I, named him George."

"Mind if I feed, George?" Jane asked.

"Go ahead, miss. Georgie seems to have taken to you and your dog. I see you have a companion for him over in the corner." Georgie's little fingers waved in the air, touching the soft curly fur around Dog's ear.

"Jane is our son's wife. Another Mrs. Bradley," Arnie added with a smile.

"Mr. Bradley, pardon me for being presumptuous, but you said you might have some work. I could help you—maybe for food, for a day or two, for me and George?"

"I think that could be worked out … for a day or two. The horse barn has a corner with a bunk, a small space heater, if you don't mind—"

"That would be fine, sir. When Georgie finishes that bottle, you just take me to the barn. I think he'll sleep while you show me what you'd like to have done."

Georgie finished his bottle and Jane, like a pro, burped him patting his back, his little head resting on her shoulder. Letting out a big belch, the baby brought a smile to everyone's face especially Arnie and Martha's. Jane was a natural with the baby.

Chapter 46

———

Tree House

WOLFE PROVED TO BE a man of his word and was easy going with the animals, Sir Charles included. Arnie watched him, testing if Wolfe really worked or just wanted to eat. Martha told Arnie she fixed an extra large potpie, and he should invite Wolfe to join the family for dinner. No doubt about it, the man was hungry. He finished his first serving of chicken-potpie eagerly accepting a second helping when Martha offered—after she offered, never presuming.

After dinner Arnie called the chief asking him to check out their visitor. Information he gave the chief was sketchy. All he could tell his friend was the man's last name, approximate height—just under six feet same as Arnie, Native or African American, maybe late thirties. And, he was carrying a four-month-old baby in a basket. Supposedly the mother had died giving birth.

Chief Saxon called Arnie back the next morning. "No one of Mr. Wolfe's description matched anyone in the wanted files, or anyone with a prior record in the past year in New Hampshire, or neighboring states. Also, I still have nothing on the skeleton."

"Thanks, Roy."

Wolfe worked hard, handling more chores almost before he was asked. By mid-October, it seemed as if he had found a home for himself and Georgie. He cared for his baby, never wanting to be a burden to any of the Bradley family.

Arnie had an idea he'd been mulling over, and this morning at breakfast, just before Jane was leaving for school, he was ready to ask her and Martha what they thought. Sipping his second cup of coffee, he glanced over at Martha. "What would you think about offering Wolfe the little house in the back of the property by the lake? He could clean—"

"Arnie, that place is uninhabitable and it's the size of a tree house. It's in no condition for anyone to live in. I don't know what your ancestors used it for, but—"

"Well, the man would have to make it livable. We'd buy the materials he required, within reason. Martha he's a good worker and we need help. Jane, I caught you lifting a crate yesterday. No more of that, young lady."

Martha sighed. "You're right. We do need help. Dog never leaves George's side or Wolfe's for that matter. A dog knows a person, knows if he can be trusted. All right, offer the tree house to him and, instead of inviting him to come to the house for dinner every night, let him know he's always welcome ... and, that starting today I'm planning my grocery list to include him and Georgie."

Chapter 47

———

"HAVE YOU NOTICED Jane lately?" Martha asked watching BigRed cruise away down the driveway.

"I noticed, well, heard her—another bout of morning sickness. Poor thing. She thought she was done with that phase. Have to hand it to her—late or not, she went to school." Arnie sat back in his chair. His wife was leading up to something.

"No, I meant, have you noticed how much she's showing. Seemed to have popped out overnight. That baby will be here before you know it. And, we have to be careful we don't ask her to do too much. She doesn't complain, but I can see how tired she is."

"Come on, Martha. Tell me what's going on under that bun of yours."

"You're not the only one with ideas." Sighing, Martha topped off her mug of coffee and then Arnie's.

"Something I can help with?" he asked, watching his wife over the rim of his mug.

"Once Jane's baby … well, let's just say maybe our grandbaby could have a playmate."

"A playmate? You wouldn't be thinking of hooking up Georgie and the baby? I think they'll be a little young to be dating."

"No, silly. Georgie's not a fussy baby. He could make a fine playmate once our grandbaby is a month or two. Wolfe could scrounge around in our attic, or the barns—God knows every spare shed, attic, corner of the farm is full of furniture that your father, back to the first Bradley, stored along the way. *They* didn't get rid of anything so we might as well put some of it to use. Anyway, I bet Wolfe could find a couple of cribs, set them up in my combination office-sewing room. It's a large room— convenient off the kitchen. He could set up one crib for Georgie now. Then Wolfe won't have to worry about him, which I know he does, hauling him everywhere. Why don't you run it by him? If he likes the idea, ask him to find a crib in one of the attics, or stashed in one of the barns ... anywhere."

"Martha, you have more than you can handle without adding babysitting—"

"Humph, I'll be babysitting when Jane has her baby so I might as well let Georgie be the warm up."

"Mind you, I think it's a great idea, but ..."

"But what?"

"I worry it might be too much for you, that's all."

"I was up in the attic yesterday, poking around. Arnie, I found a beautiful spindle crib. Could be cherry, maybe oak. It's so dusty, grimy really, I couldn't tell. I think I saw a similar one in that back barn where your grandfather left an old car. Honestly, your ancestors kept everything."

"Okay. Did you say you want to talk to Wolfe, or do you want me to?" Arnie asked pulling on his riding boots.

"How about I talk to Jane when she gets home. See what she thinks about the idea. If I'm reading her right, the way she acts with little Georgie, I think she'll be for it."

Chapter 48

———

DOG BARKED INSISTENTLY at the back door. It wasn't his usual bark—sitting, tail brushing the ground, waiting to be let in kind of bark. Martha set the greasy skillet in the sink to soak, wiped her hands on her apron, and went to see what was causing the animal's distress.

Opening the door, Dog immediately raced down the path toward the horse barn. Turning, he raced back to Martha, barking, barking, running back down the path, tongue hanging out, eyes glazed.

Dog was urging her to follow, commanding her to follow.

Martha took her jacket off the peg wrapping it around her body, warding off the chilly November air. "Okay, okay, I'm coming. Stop your barking."

Leaving the thickening gray clouds, she entered the cool shadowy barn with a scent of hay freshly stacked, ready to be pitched into Charlie's stall. Squinting in the dim light, she saw a body lying face down in front of the stallion's stall.

It was Arnie.

Screaming, she fell to her knees alongside his lifeless body pulling on his arm. "Arnie, Arnie!"

She ran outside screaming for Wolfe. "Help, help! Wolfe."

Hearing Dog's barking then Martha's scream, Wolfe came running from the chicken's pen. He knelt by Arnie, felt his neck for a pulse. "Mrs. Bradley, go, go, call for help. 9-1-1."

Wolfe turned Arnie onto his back. Placing one palm over the other, he started administering CPR, counting, screeching out the cadence with each compression.

Martha remained frozen next to her husband, strands of her hair streaked with gray falling from her bun, hair pins lost.

"Mrs. Bradley, GO FOR HELP!"

"Yes. Yes." Martha struggled to her feet, ran, staggering on shaky legs to the house.

Gripping the wall phone she dialed 9-1-1. "I need help, my husband is unconscious, Bradley Farm. Hurry. Hurry."

It was thirteen minutes, forever, before the ambulance arrived.

Martha, pacing at the top of the driveway, waved at the driver to follow her as she took off running down the path, her arms pumping to push her faster.

The ambulance bumped along over the dirt road following the stricken woman. Two medics jumped out of the van, dashed into the barn.

Wolfe backed away, his heartbeat erratic.

The first medic raced back to the van, retrieved the portable defibrillator. Ran back.

The medic leaning over the body looked up at his partner. Shook his head.

They were too late.

Arnold Bradley was dead before the first compression on his chest.

Chapter 49

———

ARNIE WAS ONE of those men who other men liked, valued, swapped stories with—a man's man. It was no surprise to Martha, or Jane, that many towns' people came to pay their last respects. Many, but not his sister or brother. They couldn't make such a sudden trip, so far away, they told Martha. So be it, Martha hung up the phone with a heavy heart.

The driveway filled with cars spilling down beyond the Bradley farm sign, down onto the grassy shoulders of the road, cars carrying the mourners. Mourners carried covered dishes, plastic-wrapped baking sheets of cookies, bowls of pasta salad, donating all manner of food for the family and guests celebrating Arnold Bradley's life.

It was the first time many of them, the majority, had seen Wolfe. Only a few knew the man was helping out on the farm. Wolfe was the subject of some of Arnie's stories—how the man had shown up one day with a baby son in a basket. How the man seemed adept at whatever task Arnie gave him.

The November day was cold but filled with sunshine. The mourners stood silently as Hank the minister spoke kindly of his friend. Arnold Bradley was laid to rest next to Marshall Bradley who bought the farm, built the farmhouse. They trooped away from the family plot, the plot on the knoll facing the lake, silently forming a line behind Martha, Jane, and Hank, entering the farmhouse through the back door.

The women set about putting the food out on the white linen tablecloth covering the dining room table. Jane switched on the cassette player, turning up the volume, filling the house with the voice of Ella Fitzgerald, John Coltrane on the saxophone, the trumpet of Miles Davis, and always Louis Armstrong, Satchmo—all favorites of Arnie's. Oh, how he loved his jazz. Tommy and Cilla stood by Jane as she lined up the cassettes, asking them to see that there was never a lull in the music, a lull that would let in the sadness of the day. She gave each a hug, thanked each for their support, then went to find Martha. She didn't dare linger with her friends for fear the sadness, the tears tamped down deep inside, would surface.

Jane hadn't received a letter from Danny in well over three weeks. She longed to hear from him. She and Martha had decided not to write to him about his father's death, hoping to ease the sad news by reassuring him with their voices that they could manage the farm. Of course, the two women did not sit idly by waiting for a letter or Danny's call. They had contacted the Army to see if Danny could fly home for his father's funeral, or, better yet, come home for good, to help his mother and wife run the farm, given the death of his father. They didn't want Danny to learn of his father's death through the Army, but perhaps a chaplain would be given the task if his mother couldn't tell him personally.

There had been no response to their request as yet. Nothing from the Army and nothing from Danny.

Jane thanked Tommy and Cilla for their help. Cilla, standing next to Tommy asked the obvious question—when is the baby due? Jane *briefly* told them how she learned of her pregnancy, *briefly* filled them in about the class she was taking at the University of New Hampshire. The three agreed to meet over the holidays for lunch … or something.

Glancing around at the people milling about, she went to the kitchen looking for Martha. As she approached Martha, cutting a chocolate layer cake with fudge frosting from one of her friends, the phone rang. Martha turned to answer it. "Yes, I'm Mrs. Bradley. No, not Jane Bradley. Hold on, Jane Bradley is right here."

"It's for you, Jane."

"Who," Jane whispered.

"He didn't say. Just asked for you."

"Hello, this is Jane Bradley."

"Hello, ma'am. I'm Captain Quinn. Your husband—"

Jane, her heart pounding glanced at Martha. *God no!*

"Ma'am are you there?"

"Yes, I'm here." Jane motioned to Martha to put her ear next to hers so she could hear.

"Your husband, his group, was hit with enemy fire—"

"Just tell me. Is he dead?" she whispered, her eyes squeezed shut.

"No, ma'am. He's alive. He received immediate aid from a medic … the medic saved him, stopped the bleeding, stabilized him. He lost his left leg. As soon as it was safe, he was evacuated by helicopter. He and the other wounded were taken to a field hospital. He'll be in Da Nang for a few more days, then transported to Japan, then to the States. Once in the U.S., he will be transported to a hospital near your home—Portsmouth, New Hampshire, for treatment. You will receive word when this will occur, but it will be a few weeks."

"Captain, when was Danny wounded? I haven't received a letter for—"

"He was hit three days ago, in the morning. You will receive a communiqué in the next two days, with a military contact regarding your husband's condition and exactly when you can expect him to arrive at the Portsmouth hospital."

Jane, eyes to the ceiling, blinked rapidly to hold the tears at bay. "Captain, my husband's father had a heart attack … three days ago. He died. Can you arrange for a chaplain to tell him? The funeral was today … it doesn't seem right that Danny doesn't know about his dad … unless you think it's better to wait until he comes home."

"Don't worry, Mrs. Bradley. Unfortunately, this has happened all too often. I'll see to it that a chaplain speaks to your husband."

"Thank you." Jane hung up the receiver. "Martha, it sounds as if Danny was wounded at the moment his father died."

Breathing in gulps, Martha's face drained of blood, leaned into Jane's loving arms. Patting Martha's back, she lifted her chin allowing the woman's head to tuck in close. "Jane, no more. No more. I can't handle any more." Her tears turned to sobs.

"It's okay, Martha. We're together," Jane said, her hand stroking her mother-in-law's back. "Together, we'll do whatever we have to."

They stood alone in the kitchen holding each other. The younger, holding the elder, began to grasp the magnitude of the last few days and the ramifications of her place as a Bradley on Bradley farm. With Martha clinging to her, had they switched places?

Chapter 50

———

THE DAYS DRAGGED as Jane waited for Danny's return to the States. Many times she ran to the chicken coop, gulping for air, swiping at the tears rolling uncontrollably down her cheeks. Clutching the bar in front of Daisy's nest, she sobbed over the loss of Arnie, over the wounds her husband had suffered, sobbed until the overwhelming feeling of helplessness passed.

Today was a new day. She had to be strong for Martha, for Danny, for herself. Gradually opening her eyes, forcing herself to get out of bed, she braced for the roiling in her stomach. She tentatively moved her legs over the side of the bed, touching her toes on the braided rug.

So far so good. No mad dash to the toilet.

A whiff of fresh brewed coffee curled beneath the door into her bedroom. It was inviting. That was different. It was the first time in a long time that she didn't have to make a run for the bathroom. Could it be her morning sickness was abating? She thought so once before only to suffer its return.

She took her time to dress not daring to move too fast. Shuffling to the oval mirror, she laid her palms on her protruding tummy. The baby bump was no longer a bump, more like a basketball. Did it grow bigger overnight? Martha had taken her shopping for maternity clothes weeks ago in preparation for the day she could no longer wear her clothes. Daughters of Martha's church friends loaned her several bags of clothes. The bags appeared out of nowhere once the word was out that Martha was expecting a grandchild.

Jane was thankful there were only a few more days of classes. By Thanksgiving she would be finished with the semester. Because of her high marks, the professor told her she was exempt from taking the finals. Should she sign up for the next course in January, or should she wait until after the baby was born—the doctor thinking mid-March. How was she going to manage? She only knew she would provide whatever he needed, she would be there for him.

Martha was looking tired, her eyes dull, mourning her husband's death, crying many nights. Jane didn't escape the sadness of Arnie's passing. She missed his smile, missed their chats grooming the horses, and especially missed his encouraging words. He was always ready to perk her up when she was feeling overwhelmed. She couldn't allow herself to think of him too often, because when she did her eyes filled with tears. She couldn't allow Martha to see this. She had to remain strong for her. Only in the night did she allow herself to think of her friend.

Dressed, holding onto the stair rail, Jane padded down the steps to the kitchen, to the ringing of the telephone. Wolfe was setting Georgie in his crib in the sewing room, Martha scrambling eggs in the skillet, so Jane answered the phone.

There was a pause. Then in a loud voice, to be sure Martha and Wolfe heard as she spoke into the receiver. "Danny. Danny, is that you?"

"Yeah, wait a minute. A nurse wants to stick a thermometer in my mouth. I don't get it. My mouth wasn't hurt."

Jane's brows drew together. Danny wasn't joking. He sounded upset, mad even.

"Danny?"

"Okay, she's coming back later."

"Where are you?"

"Portsmouth ... at least that's what they're telling me. Janie, can you come to the hospital ... today?"

"Of course. Danny, you're so close. We'll be there soon … as soon as we finish the morning chores … before lunch."

● ● ●

WALKING DOWN THE STARK white corridor to Danny's hospital room, breathing in the smell of disinfectant, Jane's stomach was in turmoil but this time not because of nausea, but filled with excitement, butterflies. She hurried ahead a few steps, Martha following close. Wolfe was last in line, pushing the stroller he found in one of the barns. Martha told him it was Danny's when he was a baby. Arnie must have put it there. He saved everything. She was happy to see it still had some value. She asked Wolfe to come to the hospital with them. Maybe it would help Danny to know there was a man around to help.

Room 18 was two more doors ahead.

Jane passed a nurse leaving the room as she ran through the open doorway, a smile spreading across her face as she stepped quickly to Danny's bedside, grasped his arm, bending to touch her lips to his. Tears streamed down her face, tears she hoped Danny would interpret as tears of joy. She'd do her best to make him think that, to hide her alarm. Danny looked emaciated, no sparkle or the usual merriment in his eyes. He looked beaten down.

Martha was on the other side of the bed babbling on, and on, thanking God that Danny was home.

Jane couldn't find words as she gripped his hand.

Martha introduced Wolfe. "We told you how Arnie … she was suddenly overcome saying her husband's name, Danny's father's name, collapsing in the chair Wolfe had placed by the bed for her.

"I'm sorry, Danny," his mother said. "I told myself not to cry, but I miss your father so much. Thank God you're home, Danny," Martha said again.

"It's okay, Mom. I wish I could have been home with you."

Wolfe pulled up another chair on the other side of the bed for Jane. Sitting on the chair, Jane made herself smile, keeping hold of Danny's hand. She held his hand to her protruding belly. "Here's your baby, Danny. Feel that little kick?"

A spark of life came to his eyes as he felt the movement under Jane's maternity smock. He glanced at Jane, his lips forming a hint of a smile that quickly faded. "Janie, I'm no good ... I can't think straight. I can't remember things. I feel numb —"

"You'll be home soon, the farm —"

"That's what I'm trying to say ... I don't care about the farm." Danny shut his eyes, turned his head away.

Jane held his hand to her cheek, a simple gesture, a lifeline.

A nurse popped her head in the door, informing them that the doctor was finishing up with a patient and then would be right in.

Wolfe tilted the chart up attached to the end of Danny's bed. Glancing at the entries, he saw Daniel Bradley was ready to be fitted for a left leg below the knee.

> Fit only. Use crutches until further notice. No physical therapy with prosthesis until the stump heals completely. Release in three days to home care as outpatient. Physical therapy with the prosthesis to be scheduled when ready. Six months to a year for recovery.

Wolfe carefully returned the chart against the foot of the bed frame. Georgie giggled banging a soft yellow duck on the stroller's tray. His daddy automatically bent down, kissed the toddler's cheek, his mind running through the ramifications of what he had just read. Danny would require help to recover from his injuries, lots of help, and more important to recovery—his will to live.

Martha dried her eyes as Jane looked from Danny to Wolfe. Locking eyes on Wolfe, her message was clear—we need your help more than ever, please stay, please help us all to recover.

Chapter 51

———

SEVERAL WOMEN IN VARIOUS stages of pregnancy sat waiting outside the doctor's office. One leaned back, earbuds in place, eyes closed. Two others were thumbing through magazines.

Jane and Martha sat side by side staring at the picture of a sailboat gliding through waves of sparkling blue water. Her mind was filled with Danny—how thin he was, stress lines carved into his face. Years were added to the man she loved in the time he had been deployed, wounded, and now home to her. Yet, it had only been a few months.

Seeing Danny yesterday had been unsettling. She desperately wanted to help, comfort him but she wasn't sure how. She exchanged a few words with his doctor before they left—how helpless she felt. What should she do? The doctor only said that Danny's state of mind was typical when a soldier returns from the front with a loss of a limb, coupled with what he witnessed on the battlefield. She should give him time.

Well, she wasn't going to settle for typical. She would bring her husband back, bring back the man the way he was before he became a soldier. Danny needed her and she was determined not to let him down. Soon to be nineteen, she was married, pregnant, with a wounded warrior she loved more than life itself. Somehow she was going to gather the strength and the wisdom to give him what he needed.

Martha needed her too. She was drowning in sorrow over the death of her husband.

"Mrs. Bradley."

Both Martha and Jane looked up, stood, followed the nurse in blue scrubs.

Jane settled on the examination table, the flowered gown open exposing her belly. She rubbed her arms to ward off the chill of the room, glancing at Martha, then back to the nurse as the doctor joined them.

"Ah, my two favorite Bradley women. Jane, how are you feeling? Anything of concern?"

"Everything seems to be fine," Jane said softly. "Except I seem to tire easily. More and more I'd say. And, it seems like I'm getting bigger every minute."

The doctor nodded as she took measurements of Jane's belly, the nurse noting the numbers on Jane's chart as the doctor gave her the information. "Hmm, your belly has grown significantly since your last visit. Tiring. Naturally I don't know for sure, but from my experience, I'd say there is a chance, a good chance, that you're carrying twins. You might want to tuck that in your mind, be prepared ... just in case."

Jane blinked at the doctor. *What did she just say?*

"Jane, did you hear me?" The doctor was smiling at her, smiling at Martha.

• • •

DRIVING HOME IN SILENCE, Jane sat behind the wheel of the station wagon. Suddenly the two women erupted in uncontrollable laughter, alternately shedding tears at the wonder she might be carrying twins. Laughed at the thought of two of everything, and then sobered at the turn of events over the past weeks.

Jane stole a glance at Martha staring out the windshield. "Do you think Danny is worried, scared about coming home?" she asked. "Yesterday, he seemed a little distant, not himself. Of course, who would be the same, after what he must have seen, and then such a severe injury ... losing ... it would be natural ... not to be himself ... knowing he won't be able to help around the farm ... for awhile. That would bother him ... a lot, don't you think?"

Martha let a sigh escape her lips. "Yes. Six months, give or take, on crutches ... Jane, I'm so glad you're his wife."

Jane stared at the road ahead, shocked at Martha's words. The woman seemed to barely tolerate her presence, although she had seen some chinks in her armor especially after her husband's death. This was the first time she embraced Jane as her son's wife. Glancing at Martha, she saw tears meandering down her cheeks before Martha wiped them away with the sleeve of her jacket.

Without thinking, Jane reached across the console for Martha's hand.

"Jane, now you have to get in touch with your parents."

"I know, and I will."

"Good. A call?"

"I think a letter. Let them get over the shock of not one grandchild, but two."

The thought of the O'Neill's reaction sent the pair into another fit of laughter. How good it was to laugh. It seemed to ease the apprehension of what was ahead.

"I have to call Cilla too. Our lives are so different—Cilla in Michigan attending the university, and me a wife expecting a baby, maybe twins."

Both sighed, silent again, lost in their own thoughts.

"Wolfe had an idea to help Danny, something creative, bring some joy to his mind."

"What was that, dear?" Martha asked.

Jane gripped the wheel with both hands, raised her chin a notch. *She said Dear. How wonderful to hear Martha's term of endearment again.* Without realizing the change, she had begun to think of Martha as a mother figure. It was comforting to know she wasn't alone, nor would she let Martha feel alone. She would be there for her as well as Danny.

"I didn't mention it before, but Wolfe remarked one day, shortly after he set up housekeeping in the tree house, that a corner of one of the barns was set up as a woodworking space."

"That's right. Danny set up the place in the barn when he was taking shop classes at school."

"Well, yesterday morning before we left for the hospital, he pulled me aside. Said he found a cradle in the rafters of the horse barn. He wondered what I thought about his mentioning it to Danny when he came home. He said the cradle needs refinishing. What do you think of his idea?"

"I think it's a capital idea, except for one thing."

"And that would be ...

Smiling through misty eyes, Martha said, "Wolfe will have to find another cradle, or Danny will have to build one. Don't forget, dear, there may be two babies on the way."

Chapter 52

———

PANCAKES DOTTED WITH BLUEBERRIES were lined up on the griddle. Wolfe sat at the kitchen table spooning baby cereal, alternating with applesauce, into Georgie's open, bird-like mouth waiting for the next spoon coming his way.

"I guess I'd better start looking around the attics, barns, and the sheds for more baby furniture," Wolfe said glancing over at Jane. "Which bedroom are you going to set up for a nursery?"

"Well, first we have to change one of the rooms downstairs for me and Danny. He won't be taking the stairs any time soon," Jane said popping a bite of pancake in her mouth.

"We can keep the sewing room as a nursery to start with," Martha said.

Jane sat at the table, two pads of paper lying in front of her, slippers kicked off, her toes wiggling in Dog's curly fur. Under the table, Dog's eyes slid side to side watching feet move from stove to refrigerator and back to the table.

"Tommy called. Word is out that Danny was wounded and is coming home. He offered to help." Sighing, Martha topped off everyone's coffee.

"Wait until he learns that Danny is going to be a father, maybe father of twins. I'll call Tommy, see if he can come over today, move the bedroom furniture down … down where, Martha?"

"How about the dining room? Wolfe, can you rework the swinging door into the kitchen so that it latches? Give Danny and Jane some privacy."

"I'll take care of the chickens this morning—haven't seen Daisy or Sir Winston for days. Her fresh eggs sure taste good with the pancakes," Jane said with a small grin.

"We need another batch of chicks. The chicken farmer down the road called, said that he would save some for us. Good price."

Jane pondered Martha's words. Chicks? More chickens wouldn't give them the income they needed. With Arnie's death, there was no more horse farm—breeding, racing, or training. A knot formed around her babies. How were they going to survive? Jane was familiar with the accounts, Martha's record keeping. Jane figured money would run out by the end of next summer.

Martha added more pancakes to the platter. "After Tommy comes over today, or tomorrow, and sets up your bedroom, Jane, let's all go together to check the barns and sheds for furniture ... with any luck we'll find some baby furniture for Danny to work on. I hope he takes to your idea, Wolfe."

The knot in Jane's belly eased. It would be fun scouting out furniture in all the buildings on the farm. She had only been in the chicken coop and the horse barn.

Suddenly Dog, nails digging into the black and white squares of the linoleum, scooted out from under the table, stretched, and trotted into the sewing room, flopping down on the braided rug beside Georgie's crib. He needed to catch some sleep while he could. He knew when the humans talked rapidly he was in for a busy day.

Chapter 53

———

TONY SCARPETTI PARKED his used army Jeep, still sporting its original camouflage paint, down the road off the shoulder from Bradley farm. He had missed one opportunity, a few days ago, to snoop around the farm. When he took up his stakeout, he realized he was too late when he witnessed the family's station wagon pulling up the driveway to the house.

Three people had exited the car, an older woman he knew by a photo taken at a church, was the senior Mrs. Bradley. He didn't know who the ponytailed man was, but he didn't look tough— skinny, a little kid in his arms. The younger woman had been identified as the new wife of Daniel Bradley who was in the Army. Now that Tony was on the case of his family's missing treasure, he scouted the newspaper every day for more articles on the bones found in the cellar of the farmhouse.

His diligence paid off. There was a news clip in the morning paper that the son was in a Portsmouth hospital, returned wounded from the fighting in Vietnam. Smirking, Tony folded the paper. He always prided himself on taking action when opportunity knocked.

Today was a new day, a new stakeout.

Tony didn't have a clear view of the house. Slinking from one bush thicket to another to get a better view, he finally had a good enough angle on the driveway so he would see the black wagon if it left. He poured the last of the coffee into the thermos cap mixing with coffee grounds in the bottom. Frowning, he made a mental note to watch how he set the coffee filter in the basket in the future. He decided when he finished drinking the coffee, if the women and the man didn't leave soon, he would abandon the mission for the day.

Returning the thermos to his backpack, he looked up just in time, catching a glimpse of the car passing his viewpoint as it turned out of the driveway heading east. He could see the driver clearly—the elder Mrs. Bradley. He could see what looked to be a white sweater on someone sitting next to the driver. The front seat blocked his view of the backseat. He thought he saw the arm of a black jacket, like the one the ponytail man wore when he saw him last.

With three in the car, Tony decided they were going to some kind of meeting and would be gone for at least an hour, if he was lucky. The cocky, youngest Scarpetti son was smart and always lucky. He would have time to case the house for the jewelry his dad said was stolen over thirty years ago. He chuckled—yeah, he knew how to take action, proved it when he lifted the painting from over the fireplace, returning it to the rightful owners—the Scarpetti family.

Tony crept closer to the house but remained hidden in the last line of bushes, waiting. He had to be sure that the car didn't return, someone returning to pick up something they forgot when leaving. Tony was smart that way.

Five minutes passed.

Tony made his move.

Sprinted to the back door, tool in hand to pick the lock.

The door wasn't locked. Stupid people … new lock and they don't even use it.

He disappeared into the house, the door banging shut behind him.

Chapter 54

———

STEPPING OUT OF THE HORSE BARN, Wolfe stretched, loosened up with several touch-the-toes. His back was tight from bending over, rubbing off the first layer of grime from the hooded antique cradle he discovered in the house attic. He wanted Danny to see the beauty of the wood without the dust caked on over the years. If Danny liked woodworking, as Jane said, he wouldn't be able to resist stripping the cradle to the wood.

Wolf's head jerked up.

What was that?

Backdoor?

Squinting, the morning sun blinding him, he must be hearing things. Dog emerged from the barn, taking up his post at Wolfe's side, a guttural growl escaping through his clenched teeth, ears back.

"Probably that darn ghost Martha's alluded to acting up again, Dog. I'll check on Georgie, and then you and I'll go check out the house."

Turning back into the barn, Wolfe quickly walked to Georgie's corner. The space heater warmed the makeshift nursery. Georgie, tucked under his blanket in the stroller was sleeping soundly, thumb in his mouth.

Wolfe hustled out of the barn lifting a shotgun from the rack installed by the first Bradley, as he was told by Martha. Slapping his thigh, Dog trotted along close to Wolfe's side.

Quietly pushing the unlatched door open, Wolfe and Dog entered the house. Wolfe, shotgun by his side, finger on the trigger, checked the dining room now repurposed as Jane's and Danny's bedroom. Checked the living room, and sewing room-nursery, returning to the kitchen.

Shrugging, he turned to leave when he heard something drop on the floor above him. Dog's ears snapped up. Another guttural growl, teeth bared. "Yup. Someone's up in Martha's room," Wolfe whispered.

The stairs leading up to the second-floor bedrooms would not give Wolfe an advantage. He would step into the line of sight of whoever was up there. Tiptoeing back to the sewing room, he quietly took the back set of stairs two at a time.

On tiptoe, he made his way to Martha's bedroom. Lifting the shotgun he spun into the doorway, pointing the long barrel of the gun at a twenty something man—a pretty Italian boy.

"Drop to the floor, fella, or my dog goes for your throat. Right, Dog?"

On cue, Dog bared his teeth, snarling, body quivering ready to spring.

"Okay, mister. Okay. I didn't take anything. Just looking."

"Yeah? We'll, see about that." With the gun aimed at the intruder's back, Wolfe picked up the receiver, tapped Chief Saxon's number kept on a card by the phone.

"You're making a mistake, mister. I done nothing wrong."

"Let's see. As far as I know, you don't live here. I guess that falls under breaking and entering."

"Hah. As I told you, I done nothing wrong. The back door was open, all I did was enter."

"Hello, Chief. Wolfe here, Bradley Farm. I'm pointing a shotgun at a man lying on the floor in Martha Bradley's bedroom. I'd appreciate your coming over to pick him up before Jane and Martha return. They're bringing Mr. Danny home today from the hospital."

"Did you get the guy's name?"

"Chief wants your name."

"Tony Scarpetti. I'm sure he's heard of my family. We're big around here," Tony said in a surly voice.

"Hear that, Chief? Why are you laughing?"

"Scarpetti he said? Long line of Scarpetti's. The families, Bradley and Scarpetti, were at each other's throats for years, or so the story goes—gambling, boozing, drugs. And to think, I'm going to make the first arrest on a breaking and entry of a punk son."

"How quick can you get here, Chief?"

"I'll be there in ten … with an officer. Just keep that gun on junior."

Chapter 55

———

A NURSE AND AN INTERN helped Danny into the car. Wolfe had laid the back seat flat, positioning pillows against the car's door frame so Danny could sit upright, his legs stretched out in front of him, the trouser of his left leg pinned up under his stump.

Martha drove as Jane, sitting in the passenger seat, her hand back over the console fished between the seats, held Danny's hand. Jane looked over the top of her seat. "Comfortable?"

Danny nodded. "Yeah ... anxious to get home."

Jane looked away. Her chest tightened. He looked gaunt, filled with despair, drained of energy. She'd never taken care of anyone before. She'd never had an injury worse than a scraped knee and now faced the one she loved with the loss of his leg. The thought was overwhelming, frightening. What if she failed? She was anxious for Danny to come home, but she also knew he was going to require care, probably a lot of care. It didn't matter how much. Somehow she would gain the strength, the wisdom to overcome her feeling of inadequacy. She forced herself to think only of the moment. Forcing herself to enter into idle banter, her breathing eased.

Jane and Martha spoke occasionally—exchanged quips, the latest gossip. They related stories about Dog, Wolfe and Georgie. They said nothing about the possibility that Jane was carrying twins. Jane decided to hold that news until Danny was in the house, eating a home cooked dinner, sipping a glass of wine. Her plan was to tell him when they went to bed. Together again. Husband and wife.

Seeing the car turn off the road, Wolfe stood waiting for them as Martha parked the car by the back door. Martha and Jane popped out of the car, hustling around as Wolfe opened the door to the back seat. Sticking his head in with a big grin on his face, Wolfe stuck his hand out to Danny.

"Welcome home, Mr. Danny."

Danny tried to smile, but the effort failed. Grasping Wolfe's hand he scooched to the edge of the seat. "Call me Danny. No need for the mister. Can you pull the crutches out? Here, on the floor."

Wolfe grabbed the pair of crutches, gave Danny a hand up to a standing position. He handed Danny one crutch, then the other. Wolfe had decided he would help the soldier but not baby him, give him some space to do things for himself.

"With all due respect, Mr. Danny, you are a veteran, a man I admire for stepping up, volunteering to serve my country. That leg will heal and, I'm sure with Jane's help, so will your heart. Now, you lead the way inside. Your mom is holding the door open letting in all this cold air," Wolfe said stepping back so Danny had room to maneuver. "Also, I may be mistaken, but I believe I caught a whiff of pot roast in the slow cooker this morning, along with all the vegetables from your farm. Again, welcome home."

● ● ●

DOG AND GEORGIE kept the adults laughing during dinner. Georgie, propped up with pillows in his high chair, decided if he had a bite of smooshed potatoes, that it was only fair that Dog have the next bite. The tot with a fist of potato let his hand dangle over the side at which point Dog, ever so delicately, licked the white stuff off the little pudgy fingers. This caused George to breakout in a fit of giggles as he reached for another clump of potatoes.

Jane stole a glance at Danny—did he find Dog's antics amusing? Was he relaxing?

Feeling Jane's eyes on him, Danny reached for her hand. She was sitting next to him around the corner from the head of the table, his father's chair. She quickly looked away feeling a tear forming. There was so much for Danny to deal with—the impact that he was the head of the family, the impact that his father was gone.

Wolfe set Georgie in the playpen pulled to the doorway of the sewing room, as Jane helped Martha clear the dishes.

"There was a bit of excitement here today while I was waiting for you to come home from the hospital."

"And … come on, Wolfe. Excitement?" Jane asked returning the butter to the refrigerator.

"Yup. I had to call Chief Saxon."

"Chief Saxon?" Martha put down the dishcloth, her eyes wide.

"Had an intruder. But Dog and I subdued him, didn't we, boy." Wolfe bent over, patted Dog's curly head. Dog was leaning against Danny's thigh but gave Wolfe's hand a lick.

"Yup, an intruder."

"Oh, dear. I didn't lock the door because you were …

"It's okay, Martha. Anyway, by the time Dog and I got in the house, the young punk was in your bedroom."

Martha started for the stairs.

"Don't worry, Martha. He didn't take anything. The officer with Saxon frisked him good. He was clean, but they hauled him to the station. Said his name was Tony Scarpetti. You should have heard the chief chuckle, Mr. Danny. Seems one of your relatives, early on, had some dealings with a Scarpetti. Must have been a regular Hatfield and McCoy kinda feud. The chief said he'd keep you posted why the young Scarpetti felt the need to stir the pot after all these years."

● ● ●

STANDING IN THE DOORWAY of the dining room, crutches tucked under his armpits, Danny looked at the transformation to a bedroom.

Jane turned on the bedside lamps. "The nurse gave me instructions on how to care for your leg. I have everything laid out by the lamp—gauze, ointment, bandages."

Danny swung into the room closed the door. "Janie, how am I ever going to handle the farm? I can't …

"You will. I know you will. Your home, Danny. I know things are different, but there's one thing that's the same. I love you. I love you Daniel Bradley. I will need your help soon, your support and strength, so you must let me help you now. We're a team, a team working together."

"Janie, I'm … " Danny's chin rested on the neck of his sweater, mouth open releasing a stream of air, unable to go on.

"You are my husband, Danny—my wonderful, warm, loving husband. That's what you are. Now, sit on the edge of the bed so I can dress your incision, help you into your pajamas. Then we're going to lie in this bed, hold each other, and be thankful that you are here so we can hold each other again."

"Hold each other? I wake up, thrashing, thinking, thinking, remembering when I was hit, the pain … I try not to think, remembering brings it back … I won't talk about it … don't ask me to talk about it."

Jane turned to the bed, telling herself to breathe deep, breathe deep, telling herself not to lose control, telling herself to be strong for her husband.

Danny shook his head, swung to the bed and did what Jane asked him to do. She didn't skip a beat uncovering his stump, gently applying the salve. She stood between his legs, bending to pull up his pajama bottoms. Feeling a kick, she gently took his hands in hers, holding them to her belly.

Jane put her hands on his shoulders as he moved his fingers feeling the movement. "Wow, I think there's a field goal kicker in there," he said looking up into her eyes, tears meandering down her cheeks.

"Ah, make that two field goal kickers."

"What? Two?" he laughed.

A laugh.

Short but a laugh nonetheless.

A spark in his brown eyes?

Danny grasped her cheeks, pulled her lips to his.

How wonderful to have her Danny back ... at least for the moment. She'd work hard to return the whole man to her and their babies.

Chapter 56

———

THEY SAT ON CRATES chatting in the small barn set up for woodworking. It was as if Danny and Wolfe had known each other for years. The air was crisp with the clean scent of wood soap.

Danny's crutches were propped against the barn's weathered pine boards, overalls pinned over his stump. He picked up a paintbrush, dipped it in wood cleaner laced with linseed oil. He had decided to keep the original red buttermilk paint on the hooded cradle Wolfe rescued from the farmhouse attic.

"What's your story, Wolfe … before you came to the farm?"

"Well, my dad was Army all the way. He enlisted during World War II. Times were poor, we were poor, but the Army pay was regular. He was killed in an ambush, the German invasion of Poland—a young guy in the wrong place at the wrong time.

"My mom wasn't prepared—a widow at thirty-one with me, a ten-year-old. We were still reeling from the depression. History books say the depression ended in '39. Let me tell you, we felt it long after. I grew up doing odd jobs—helped a plumber, spent time in a wood finishing shop and a gas station with a garage to fix cars. Whenever I applied for a job, I'd always say I was an experienced apprentice—whatever they needed.

"I married like you—young. We never had a baby," Wolfe chuckled. "It wasn't for the lack of trying. We loved each other. All of a sudden, a little over a year ago, she got pregnant."

"Where is she? Here? Janie never …

"Died in childbirth. Lost my wife and my mom two months apart. Mom had stomach cancer. Brutal. If I can help you, Danny, please ask. With my mom, I practically have a degree in nursing."

Danny bent his head. "I'm asking for your help, Wolfe. Janie is my life. The light of my life." Danny pulled out a dog-eared photo from a thin leather sheath. He turned his hand so Wolfe could see—a pretty girl with perky red curls and eyes that looked like green gemstones, a green and white dotted dress flipping around her knees. She was smiling out at him.

Wolfe shook his head. "Sweet girl."

Danny put the photo back in the sleeve. "When I got hit, I was sure I was going to die. I kept seeing Janie dancing around in my head, like this picture. She saved me. Honest to God, Wolfe, when I felt those little babies kicking in her belly last night ... let's just say I'm not too proud to ask for your help. Those kicks kind of put everything in perspective—this stump is not going to define me."

"Now you're talking, Mr. Danny." Wolfe handed Danny a pad of steel wool to rub off the last layer of grime loosened by the oil.

"I don't know how we're going to make this farm work, Wolfe, but with the two of us maybe we have a chance."

Danny didn't comment on the brochure about organic gardening that Janie left on their bureau, but it got him to thinking.

"I have an appointment tomorrow at the hospital. My prosthetic is ready and the doctor and his nurses are primed with instructions. Can you come with Jane and me? When they tell me what I have to do, they're going to be of a mind I'm coming to the hospital every other day for therapy. Janie isn't strong enough to hold me and I wouldn't' ask her to anyway with the job she's preparing to perform. But you could."

"You bet I can. We'll take a look at the gym equipment, the therapy tank I believe they call it. We can work up something in this barn, don't you think?" Wolfe said handing another pad of steel wool to Danny.

"As you say, you bet we can." Danny leaned forward, slapped Wolfe's palm, touched knuckle to knuckle, both grinning like school boys—one soon to turn twenty, the other thirty something.

Chapter 57

———

CHIEF SAXON TURNED up the thermostat. It didn't help much. The police station's conference room remained cold and musty. Jane and Martha buttoned up their coats. Wolfe kept Georgie bundled in his snowsuit tucking him in the stroller with a blanket. Saxon apologized for the chill, but they didn't conduct many conference meetings.

The chief had called the farm informing Martha Bradley that young Scarpetti's father was in the station pleading his son's case as a stupid kid's prank.

The chief also told her that Scarpetti senior had an interesting story, and if Martha or anyone in the family, including Wolfe, wanted to hear it firsthand they would be welcome to come to the station, provided they arrive in the next thirty minutes.

Martha accepted the invitation. On the way to the station, Martha, with Jane's help, filled Danny and Wolfe in on the theft of the painting. Danny completed the tale with the history of the piece—mainly that his grandfather won it in a poker game.

Everyone in the car was now eager to hear the so called *interesting story*, and were now seated around the dinged conference table. Danny whispered to Jane that the table looked like it came from one of their barns.

The meeting proceeded in earnest after the introductions, when Vincenzo Scarpetti asked that his son's fine of five hundred dollars, that Saxon had slapped on Tony, be reduced, or canceled altogether.

Saxon wouldn't go that far, but asked the Bradley family for their opinion, seeing how Tony had broken into their house—didn't matter the door was unlocked, he was not invited in.

"Tony, why don't you tell the Bradley family just why you were in their home," the chief said sitting back in an old oak chair, his arms crossed over his ample chest.

"I was looking for the jewelry that one of the old Bradley thieves stole from my family, sometime in the 1940s."

Danny, mimicking the chief, leaned back in his chair, arms crossed over his chest, crutches set back against the wall. "Come on, 1940? My Grandfather Bradley?"

"Yeah, one of those. Your grandfather. He weaseled his way into the Scarpetti family, *my family*, gaining their trust. You probably don't want to hear what he did, not with the chief sitting here. But it's safe to say your grandpappy stole stuff from us. Grandfather Scarpetti disappeared before my family discovered what your grandpaps had done. I was just looking for what rightly belongs to the Scarpetti family. Jewelry worth thousands, millions by now."

"That is preposterous. My husband, Arnold Bradley never mentioned anything of the sort about his father, Mason Bradley, and I certainly don't have jewelry worth thousands in my jewelry box."

Saxon spoke up. "Mr. Scarpetti, why does your son think the jewelry might be in the Bradley farmhouse? Why don't you tell them the story you told me."

"It was the newspaper article, several months ago, in the Boston Globe. The clip about the skeleton uncovered in the Bradley's root cellar. I put two and two together. My father disappeared. He disappeared at the same time the diamonds went missing."

Vincenzo leaned forward, elbows on the table. "I figured there might be a connection because a friend of mine stopped at the farmhouse, saw the painting that Bradley stole from us—hanging right over the fireplace."

Martha jumped to her feet. "So you're the one who stole—"

"No, I did," Tony said. "As evidence that your family killed my grandfather and buried him in the—"

"Shut up and sit down, Tony," Vincenzo Scarpetti said grabbing his son's arm.

"I'll sue you, Mr. Scarpetti, your whole family, unless you return that painting. My husband's father won it in a poker game—"

"Wait just a minute, Mrs. Bradley—"

"No, you wait a—"

"Okay, folks. Calm down. Mr. Scarpetti, seeing how your son just admitted he stole the painting, I think you might want to settle the issue of the painting here and now or I'll have to hold your son for theft."

"I want that painting, Mrs. Bradley. I have to admit I heard about that poker game. How about I buy it from you?"

Martha yanked her chair away from the table, arms crossed. "I accept your offer, Mr. Scarpetti, as long as you have it appraised. And ... that you agree in front of Chief Saxon that you will send me a certified check for the appraised value, along with a *notarized* appraisal document."

"You drive a hard bargain, Mrs. Bradley. Okay, I agree ... to what you said ... if, and this is non-negotiable, if Chief Saxon drops all charges against my son for his efforts to bring the painting back in the Scarpetti family." Vincenzo turned, looked at Saxon waiting for his reply.

"There will be no charges unless Mrs. Bradley brings them," Saxon said.

Scarpetti nodded at Saxon and then Martha. Martha glared back at him.

Danny and Wolfe looked at each other, shrugging.

"Well, Mrs. Bradley? Do you agree or not?" Vincenzo asked.

"I agree I won't press charges ... AFTER ... the check and notarized appraisal are in my hand and not a minute before."

"Okay, now that the painting issue is agreed to I have one stipulation. Mr. Scarpetti you send the check to me along with the appraisal document. I will then give it to Mrs. Bradley. Now, Mr. Scarpetti, back to the matter of your accusation about your father being buried in the root cellar."

Scarpetti sighed. "I brought a picture of him." Vincenzo opened a briefcase removing an eight by ten frame with a picture of four people.

Tony jumped to his feet. "Grandpa Scarpetti is the heavyset man on the left. I bet you anything that … that Mason Bradley killed him and buried him that cellar."

"That is the most ridiculous thing I've ever heard." Martha shot up to her feet again, hands on the table staring daggers at Vincenzo Scarpetti.

The chief, knowing about the feud between the two families had to restrain himself from laughing. "Let me see that picture, Mr. Scarpetti. Hmm, just how tall would you say your father was? I can see he was heavyset and that's being kind."

"He was a big guy, held his own. At least six foot three."

"I see. Six-foot-three. Heavy. I can tell he has large bones. I'm very sorry to have to tell you Mr. Scarpetti, much as you would like to believe the skeleton is your relative, it is not. The skeleton found in the cellar of the farmhouse was of a person no more than five-foot-eight and the bones are not those of a heavy person."

Chapter 58

———

THE FIRST SNOW of the season, early though it was, began dusting the farm with lacy ice crystals. Martha was at the stove stirring a pot of chicken stew thick with carrots, potatoes and snippets of her favorite herbs from the summer garden. She kept several strings of herbs hanging on the side porch to dry, ready to spice up whatever she was cooking.

Jane lit four candles in brass holders on the kitchen's long table, a table Martha and Arnie were going to replace last year with a smaller one Martha spotted in the attic. She was glad they never did as the household had grown with people and activity—Wolfe and Georgie, and then in March, only a few months away, the baby, or babies, would arrive. In fact, she was going to ask Wolfe to scout around in the barns for a harvest table, bigger than the table they now had in the kitchen.

Turning the music up on the radio, Jane hummed along as she added the silverware to the place settings. Martha dished out the steaming stew into large bowls, Jane setting them at each person's place.

Wolfe topped off the wine glasses. Jane added the last of a bottle of seltzer water to her glass.

The kitchen filled with the scent of freshly baked bread on a cutting board next to Danny. Cutting the loaf into thick slices, he set them in the basket to pass around the table. The bread was followed by soft butter and raspberry jam that Martha and Jane put up at the end of summer. Jams, jellies, pickles—the preserves a part of Jane's training to be a farmer's wife.

There wasn't much chatter, each filled with their own thoughts following the day's activities.

Martha leaned back in her chair, savoring a sip of wine. Looking over the rim of her glass, her eyes fixed on Danny, then Jane. "The farm isn't doing well. In fact the last of the breeding income, Arnie's last couple of months, will only tide us over until February. The bank won't extend our credit."

Her voice was soft. No loud declaration of bankruptcy, or of a pending foreclosure for lack of funds to make payments on two mortgages. Three pairs of eyes lifted slowly from the bowls of chicken stew. Jane and Danny sought each other's eyes, and then turned to Martha.

Jane was aware it was only a matter of time. Looking at the farm's books, preparing her class assignments with Martha, incorporating what she had learned into the farm's accounts. The result was obvious. Even following her professor's lectures with better methods to analyze a business, making changes to the figures—nothing changed the result. Still, it was a shock to hear the words. Solving class business problems ceased to be a matter of an assignment. Solving the farm's money problems, keeping it from going under, was real.

"Breeding racehorses is over," Martha added. "We can't maintain the farm. It's unsustainable."

Jane nodded. Yes, they were blessed. Danny was home and babies were on the way, but something had to be done about the farm. She feared they were going to lose it. She had an idea that would bolster their income. Her eyes darted to her husband, darted to Martha. She couldn't stop herself. "I have an idea. Actually it's something I've thought about driving back and forth to school."

No one spoke.

Martha shot a look at Jane, a dismissive look that said, *it's okay, dear. You just concentrate on your babies.*

Danny and Wolfe sighed in unison. They both knew the farm was hurting, but ... February?

Jane's heart pounded in her chest, air stuck in her lungs. She couldn't believe she spoke so grandly, like she had a solution. But, she believed she did.

Jane plunged on.

"An idea for a different kind of farm. Christmas trees to start with."

Still no one spoke, but Martha had an unusual look on her face this time, something sparking in her head.

"Arnie planted about a hundred sapling fir trees a few years back. Remember, Danny, he joked that if times got tough we could weather the lull with Christmas trees. Do you suppose those trees are mature enough—what, five to seven feet tall?"

"Sounds about right, Mom."

"Dog and I were down by the road, trudging through those rows of trees a few days ago. I'd say they're about right ... for a family Christmas tree."

Danny looked at Wolfe. "We could change the sign, paint out the word *horse*, hang a slat underneath, *Christmas Trees*." Danny waved his hand like he was writing the words.

"Yup, we could easily do that."

"And hang another slat beneath the tree one—*Antiques*." Jane's eyes were skipping from one to the other. "We can haul out some of the old stuff in storage from the original owners—an antique's farm. We have all the raw materials, all we need is some elbow grease Well, lots of elbow grease."

Martha stood, hands on her hips, paced from stove to table, picked up the empty plates in a stack, placed them in the sink. She looked at the ceiling, talking to no one in particular. "The farm is full of antiques—attic, barns, sheds."

Wolfe leaned his chair back, nodded slowly, leaned forward. "They sure are full of something, Martha. We could sort through, set out items that only needed to be cleaned to start. It would take too much time to refinish anything for the holidays, besides people like to refinish their own antiques ... some people do."

The holidays!

They froze in place. Alarm spreading across their faces.

No one had thought of the upcoming holidays.

Buying season!

Could they be ready?

Wolfe was on his feet, looking out the kitchen window, his mind full of the stuff he saw. He didn't notice the combination of panic and excitement that crossed the other's faces when he called up the holidays. "I saw many kerosene lamps packed away, discarded in boxes. There are kits now. Could electrify 'em. Probably best to leave the lamps as is. Jane, we don't have a shop—"

"The small barn, near the road. We could put the initial items there. Nothing fancy. Test the market."

Danny laughed, leaned over, tipped her chin up planting a quick kiss on her cheek. "Two classes at the university and you're a whiz kid at business."

"Daniel Bradley, are you making fun of me?"

"Not in the least. I think your ideas are great. Definitely worth trying."

Martha stopped pacing beside her son's chair. "Danny, you have to be careful. You have strict instructions on wearing that bionic prosth ... prosthesis, only an hour at a time, and crutches in the snow won't—"

"I can do a lot. Besides, Wolfe is setting up a regular therapy tank in the horse barn. I first suggested the small barn with the workshop, but I said it would be more fun to talk to Mildred and Charlie, you know, counting my sit-ups. So, I have more time. No going to the hospital except to check on my progress."

"So called therapy tank, Mr. Danny. That bar above the stall door, across from Mildred, is ready—get that upper body strong."

"Mom, which shed did Dad put that snowmobile in? That sure was a good year—he bought several toys."

"I saw some sets of china when I first poked around the attic in the house. Some are hand painted. Bring everything to be washed to the kitchen. I'll make them sparkle, take them down—"

"Oh, no you won't, sweetheart. Wolfe and I will take care of the taking up and down. And, no lifting for you."

Jane beamed at her husband, her eyes warm with love, a hint of a tear slipped over her lower lid.

Danny thought he said something wrong. "What?"

"I love you," Jane said getting up, standing in back of Danny's chair, wrapping her arms over his shoulders. She hadn't heard him call her *sweetheart* since the day he left for Fort Benning.

Her husband had come back to her.

Chapter 59

————

THE STRATEGY SESSION went into the wee hours of the morning. Tasks added to lists, tasks moved from one list to the other. Lists were crumpled up, discarded into the blazing fire, flames dancing merrily to the tune of the frenzy circling the living room. Every two hours Danny insisted that Jane take at least a twenty-minute nap.

Dog lay in front of the fire resting up for what was to come. Crutches were in reach as Danny from time to time swung into the kitchen to start a fresh brew of coffee.

Finally, satisfied they had a game plan, Jane stood rubbing her lower back. Danny took her hand pulling her to him, positioning her back, her hips so he could massage the knots away.

"I, for one, am heading to bed," Martha said, yawning. "Wolfe, no need to disturb Georgie. It's one o'clock. You bunk in the bedroom at the top of the stairs. You'll hear him if he wakes up. Jane, what time do you want to hit the attic?"

"Sevenish? Okay with you? We'll need a good breakfast first."

"I'll take care of the chickens," Wolfe said.

"Danny, promise me you'll not strain your leg. Don't wear that robot contraption too long."

"Don't you worry, Martha. I'll keep an eye on him," Wolfe said poking the embers, stirring the ashes.

Danny laughed. "Robotic contraption! I like that, Mom. A few more months, and I'll be ready to spring into action. You just watch me."

● ● ●

DAWN.

Adrenalin coursed through the veins of the transformers springing out of their beds. Everyone talked at once over breakfast—throwing out additional ideas, combining tasks. Georgie's eyes followed the movement of the big people, feeding Dog a bite of pancake then popping another bite with maple syrup into his own sticky mouth.

Chatter remained at a fever pitch, as dishes were cleared, everyone stoked, ready to tackle their projects. The playpen was squeezed into a spot in the attic as the women opened box after box, pulling the contents out, sorting what they found to one box or the other. Notes were written on the sides of the boxes, hinting at the contents. YES in capital letters meant Wolfe should carry the box down to the kitchen. NO meant shove the box to the side to be dealt with later. An old fainting couch was dusted off allowing Jane period respites.

By noon Danny had cut the slats, painted them, and stenciled the words ready to be secured to the Bradley Horse Farm sign at the bottom of the driveway. Wolfe picked Danny up at his workshop, transferred the slats and cans of paint colors to paint over the old sign to read, Bradley Farm, and secure the new slats beneath—Christmas Trees, Antiques. Before climbing into the truck, Wolfe helped Danny attach the prosthetic leg, and then the pair bumped up the path in BigRed, and down the driveway to complete the signage task.

After lunch, Martha and Jane put their heads together to write the copy for the ad to run in the weekend edition of several newspapers in the surrounding towns. Their first attempt at marketing the farm, something Arnie had taken care of in the past, or not, depending on racing seasons.

Wolfe and Danny, an expert at swinging around on his crutches when needed, cleaned out the small barn close to the road destined to be the antique shop. Wolfe scrubbed layers of grime caked on the wide pine floorboards from lack of use over the years. Items were either taken to the dump or put to the side for possible sale. Martha and Jane put up jams and jellies most nights after dinner, falling into bed. That task never seemed to be complete, remaining on the list.

Thanksgiving came and went. The only observance was a turkey dinner—no side dishes. Fresh baked bread for sandwiches would do this year. After Danny carved the turkey into slices, Martha insisted they pause to thank the Lord for returning Danny from the war, to keep Jane and the babies safe, thankful that Wolfe walked into their lives, and remembering the departed— Arnie. Martha paused, eyes closed, adding a special request—the strength to put a dent in the to-do lists before Christmas, mid-December if possible, to open the new business in some shape or form.

● ● ●

THE SECOND WEEKEND in December, ready or not, Bradley Farm, Christmas Trees, and Antiques was open for business.

Two of Danny's high school buddies, college boys home on break, volunteered to help with the Christmas trees, and hauling additional antiques to the new shop, the little barn by the road. Jane was under strict instructions to stay in the house, off her feet as much as possible, but she could rest in the living room or kitchen by the telephone to answer questions about the farm's new business. The most frequent question: what time was the Christmas tree lot open, and could they cut it themselves to show the children what an old fashioned Christmas was like?

Martha tied her money apron on, taking charge of all transactions. She picked her station—the antique barn near the space heater.

Epilogue

March 1971

WHERE HAD THE TIME GONE?

With a modicum of success in the transformation of the farm, they had managed to keep up with the bills. While the future didn't look easy, they thought they had a chance at making a success of the new business.

The doctor's deduction was spot on. Twin babies arrived two weeks early—a girl and a boy. Danny said it was because they wanted to get in on the action. The baby boy was named Marshall after his great, great, great grandfather Marshall Bradley who bought the land and built the farmhouse. The baby girl was named Sadie—a name Jane had always loved. When she found the origin of the name depending on which book she read—Hebrew, Spanish, English—they all agreed it meant princess.

There wasn't an hour that Jane didn't count her blessings for having Martha in her life. Her mother-in-law, counselor, and confident, was wonderful with the babies. She always knew just what to do, taking charge when the twins overwhelmed Jane. Jane was sure she was killing them when they screamed only to see them settle down when Martha handed her a warm bottle, keeping another for the other twin.

Regarding the business of the farm, Jane worried that Martha would think ill of her, think she was taking over, when at the end of the day or week she made entries into the farm's accounting books. But Martha surprised her, telling Jane she was more than happy to step back for the new generation, and felt blessed that her home was filling with babies.

Her parents had called. They were coming to visit, anxious they said, to see their two grandchildren. After their call, Jane retreated to the bedroom, tears falling nonstop. Maybe they had come to accept the life she had chosen, the husband she loved above all else. Whatever happens when they visit, she was going to try to make amends, try to help them understand how and why she loves the farm.

There was so much she and Danny planned to do.

Taking advantage of the GI bill, Danny signed up for classes, learning the new tricks of organic farming. Plus embracing his renewed passion for woodworking, he had signed up for correspondence courses on refinishing furniture, and how to recognize an antique in the first place.

Finally feeling at ease, he sat in his father's chair, head of the family, head of Bradley Farm.

Jane put her next class on hold—maybe in the fall she would be ready.

Wolfe kept on doing whatever was needed to keep the farm going—which kept him busy along with his toddler son. Georgie was fascinated with the two babies, piling his toys around them, snatching a favorite back, chastising Suzy if she ran off with one of the squeakers, her favorite kind of toy.

Jane and Danny had matured beyond their years since they were married. Jane reveled in the warmth of their home and the love of her husband and children. There would be more babies, of that she was sure.

She closed her eyes tapping the rocker blade of baby Sadie's cradle, looking into the future. Bradley Farm was given a new life, but Jane was far from finished.

She had a dream.

She dreamed of the resurgence of the barns into business centers—fresh produce in spring through fall, another for decorations in the winter—decorations year round. She had to look into how to make candles. The same barn would offer homemade products like jam, breads, pickles—wine someday? Hmm.

Over the next year she hoped they could spruce up at least one of the barns, and paint the house a sunny yellow, and add more slats to the sign with the new business centers.

The dream was clear in her mind—the transformation of the farm into a local, as well as tourist destination for holiday food, holiday decorations, antiques, and new furniture that Danny could build in one of the larger barns, dedicated to his workshop.

Jane and Danny stared at the fire. "Danny, let me paint a picture for you ... a fire is crackling with fresh pine logs, spitting sparks against the fire screen. You turn off the lamp, leaving the living room in the cozy warmth of the hearth. The colored lights on the Christmas tree twinkle—"

"I see it, sweetheart. The children in their beds and I'm in my cap holding you ... that's us, Janie. Our dream."

The End

Bradley Family Tree

Marshall Bradley
1810-1880

|

Kenneth Bradley
1845-1920

|

Mason Bradley
1896 1946

|

Arnold Bradley
1927-

|

Daniel Bradley
1951-

Author's Note

Bradley Farm

Jane and Danny dream of a houseful of children, children to help transform the homestead into a thriving business, a treasure trove of unique gifts—dried herbs and plants, jams and jellies, holiday decorations, antiques—for friends, town's people, and tourists.

They nurture their children with strong values and a good moral compass. But, as the siblings reach their thirties, will the family values be strong enough to cope with what life throws at them? Will they remain close to the homestead?

As adults, each child's story will unfold in a separate book. The books are coming—it may take awhile. After all, life is to be savored—you can't rush it.

Acknowledgements

Thank you all for your honest opinions and support. This time around it was especially helpful with character relationships, or non-relationships, whichever the case may be.

Peggy Keeney—for hanging in there with me. Your keen eye and astute viewpoint are invaluable. You always come up with the unexpected making me think, question.

Molly Tredwell—for your constant support and big picture perspective dragging the emotion out of story, and this time spotting errors in timeline.

Jay Tredwell—for your help in bringing the dogs to life.

Roger and Pat Grady—for your suggestions and honest assessments. I appreciate your time spent on my projects.

Lorna and Joe Prusak—for your valuable insight into life on a farm and your continued support.

REVIEW REQUEST

If you have the time, it would mean a lot to me if you wrote a review—what did you like best about the book? Go to Amazon. Log in. Search: Mary Jane Forbes Bradley Farm Book 1.

Thank you!

ADD ME TO YOUR MAILING LIST

Please shoot me an email to be added to my mailing list for future book launches: MaryJane@MaryJaneForbes.com Website: www.maryjaneforbes.com/

NEXT BOOK IN SERIES
Sadie, Bradley Farm Series Book 2

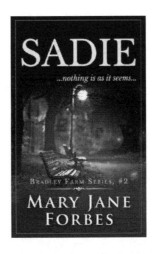

An undercover journalist. A homegrown menace. Can she break the story before terror takes hold?

Down-and-out reporter Sadie is desperate for her next gig. When she sees a job posting with an ongoing criminal investigation, she pushes aside her reservations and goes deep undercover. A group of dodgy troublemakers at the local homeless shelter seem to fit the suspect profiles, but her gut tells her there's something more to their story.

When the group's handsome leader recruits her for a dangerous secret mission, her heart skips a beat. With dreams of a Pulitzer dancing around her keyboard, she has no choice but to help plant the seeds of homegrown terrorism to keep the ruse going. After her investigation takes an explosive turn for the worse, how much will she risk to break her story before innocent lives are lost in the wreckage?

Sadie is the second standalone mystery novel in the thrilling Bradley Farm family saga series. If you like tenacious heroines, villains plucked from the headlines, and romance tinged with danger, then you'll love Mary Jane Forbes' exhilarating tale!

BRADLEY FARM SERIES

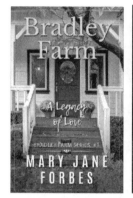

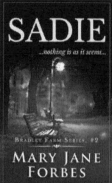

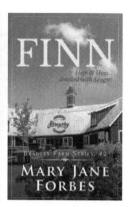

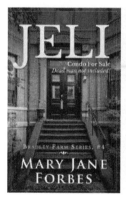

Made in the USA
Columbia, SC
06 August 2019